Sugar Rush

Julie Burchill has been a celebrated and controversial journalist since the age of seventeen, when she began writing for the *New Musical Express*. She has written for many magazines and newspapers, including *The Face*, the *Guardian* and *The Times*. She is also the author of many books, including her autobiography, *I Knew I Was Right*, a biography of Diana, Princess of Wales, and an exploration of the footballing phenomenon David Beckham, *Burchill on Beckham*. *Sugar Rush* was Julie Burchill's first novel for teenagers. It was adapted for television in 2005 by Channel 4.

Also by Julie Burchill

Sweet

Praise for *Sugar Rush*

'A fabulous story of sexual fascination – guilt-free, intoxicating and delicious. Sugar herself is a marvellous creation – promiscuous, immoral, manipulative, terrifying and oddly likeable. I only wish I'd known her when I was her age and had the chance to be tossed aside like a used condom. But who am I kidding? She'd have scared me half to death'

Melvin Burgess

'It may well be the first novel written by a 45-year-old teenager'

Toby Young, *Mail on Sunday*

'It's immediately clear that she's found her natural voice'

Tracey MacLeod, *Marie Claire*

'Hugely enjoyable'

Donald Clarke, *Irish Times*

'The best thing Julie Burchill's ever written. With this book, she's really found her voice, along with that of teenagers everywhere'

Dr

'Wonderfully realistic. Reading it on the bus is not recommended, unless you enjoy laughing like an idiot in a public place, as happened to this 16-year-old reviewer'

Luisa Gottardo, *DIVA*

'I really enjoyed *Sugar Rush* as I thought it discussed issues and ideas that would not usually be discussed in a non-poncy way. I think in this book Julie Burchill writes in a very honest and beautiful way as she talks about things I have thought about but never read before'

Sally, aged 17, Manchester

Julie Burchill

Sugar Rush

MACMILLAN

First published 2004 by Young Picador

This edition published 2016 by Macmillan Children's Books
an imprint of Pan Macmillan
20 New Wharf Road, London N1 9RR
Associated companies throughout the world
www.panmacmillan.com

ISBN 978-1-5098-0540-2

1 3 5 7 9 8 6 4 2

A CIP catalogue record for this book is available from
the British Library.

Typeset by Intype Libra Limited
Printed and bound by CPI Group (UK) Ltd, Croydon CR0 4YY

To Scarlet, Bliss and Angel
– the brilliant, beautiful Moore sisters –
from their wicked godmother

1

We got shown this film the other day at school – *Stand By Me*, it was called. It's about these boys who find a dead body and then they're all talking about whether Goofy was a dog or not.

Saint kicked me under the desk and whispered, 'Realistic, d'you know wha'mean?'

'About as realistic as your black accent!' I whispered back. She gouged my upper right thigh and I yelped and got sent out. I had to buy her a packet of Marlboro Lights to make her talk to me on the way home.

''Sides, I am black. You should'na said that.'

'Saint. You're black like Samantha Mumba's black. No one's ever got on your case about it and you're too pretty for anyone to see anything but that when they look at you. You picked up that voice off Jerry Springer and it just sounds weird.'

'Look, I'm black, you effing stupid white girl. You don't know a thing.'

She grabbed the fags and walked on ahead. I looked around for someone else to walk home with; I was just crossing the road to give Chloe Feinstein the pleasure of my company, when Saint yelled out, 'Oi, white trash! Lewis! Get your sad ass over here!'

I shrugged sorry at Chloe, who didn't look in the least surprised. What Saint wants, Saint gets, and that's just a fact – like the world being flat or double physics being boring. I was back across Surrendon Road in a flash, but Saint still made mean, narrow eyes at poor Chloe.

'What you want to hang around with that thing for? Always smells of last month's period, know wha'mean?'

I tried not to laugh, but Saint put her tongue in my ear and I couldn't help it

'Lesbos!' shouted a boy from Varndean Comp, whizzing by on a bike.

'In your dreams, trailer trash!' she yelled back. She stopped to light up, signalling to me to hold her books, and somehow forgetting to ask for them back as we continued into deepest, darkest Preston Park.

Preston Park is this suburb of Brighton where I live. You think of Brighton and you immediately think of all sorts of skanky, sleazy stuff: gay bars, all-night clubbing, people having sex on the shingle. But for all the caring parents who brought us down here from the smoke, the dream was so different. Sheltered from London – Sin City – by the rolling Downs, they believed that here their little darlings would be able to grow up in their own time, at their own pace, and never embarrass Mom and Pop in front of the neighbours by running into the house one shining summer's day waving a blown-up, lividly red and ridged condom and crying gleefully, 'Look at my balloon!'

Of course, Brighton wrote the book on sex – and the rude bits were on every single page. But Preston Park, and the other places inside the city limits that try to be like it, is, like, in denial. The wide, tree-lined streets, the manicured lawns behind the low walls – the low walls themselves a boast of affluent confidence, since it goes unwritten that nobody who walks these clean streets could ever have criminal motives – and in summer the shimmering effect of the sprinkler systems, so that life seems to be seen in soft-focus slo-mo, murmur smugly that this is a proper, proper suburb, landlocked and solid. Not the tacked-on annexe of some fly-by-night seaport. Oh no, never!

To me, Saint is like Brighton. She's the beauty and the beast. We call her Saint because it's sarky – she's been smoking twenty Marlboro Lights a day ever since we can all remember, she has sex twice a week and, though she's basically kind, she can be mean to the hangers. But on the other hand, she's Saint because she's got it all sorted, she's the shining example our parents hold out to us when we annoy them: 'Why can't you be like Zoe Clements? She never gives her parents a moment's worry!' ('Saint' Clements, geddit?) Well, Dad, that's probably because she's extremely clever and devious and lives a double life, even more than most teenagers; even though she smokes a pack a day she runs so fast and trains so hard she's in with a chance for the next Olympics, and even though she spends her evenings talking on the phone or screwing in the park she's a shoo-in for Oxford.

Even the sex thing is typical Saint. She's been doing it since she was twelve and three-quarters, but always with the same boy, and always using the Pill and condoms. (With a future that bright and a major aversion to abortion, you'd be phobic about pregnancy too.) With sickeningly symmetrical perfection, the boy she's doing the nasty with is half-black, half-white, like her, except he's got a black mum, white dad. And yes, he's really smart and nice and he looks like Craig David. And he's called Ben. Like, ahhh. (Which somewhere along the line becomes ughhh.)

Don't mind me, I'm just jealous – not about the boyfriend, just about the sortedness of it all. It seems that one moment I was this little kid only caring about animals and flowers and stuff, and then the next minute I was this raging stew of hormones. I don't know if you've ever been a raging stew of anything, but I wouldn't particularly recommend it. Being blonde, pop-eyed and pouty doesn't help an awful lot either – think Reese Witherspoon sawn off at the knees with her mush pressed against a window-pane – and throw in the fact that I'm the last fifteen-year-old virgin left in captivity and you've got a recipe for, if not disaster then certainly dismay and a fair amount of confusion.

And the dreams! Sometimes I swear I wake up blushing.

But, curiously, I'm not jealous about Ben. I'd like a boyfriend – so long as I didn't have to have sex, spend time with him or be seen with him. I'd like a boyfriend because then that side of my life would be sorted and it would be one less hurdle to be worrying about when I wake up in the morning. Sometimes this last year, it seems like I spend my life with my heart in my mouth and my stomach somewhere around my ankles, always waiting to take some high jump, be it to do with school, home, my future, sex, whatever. Except they're all invisible, and you don't hear the clatter of failure. It just comes back to haunt you much, much later, when it's too late to do anything about it.

Saint's so not like that. She approaches her life like the brilliant little ice skater she used to be – chin up, eyes straight ahead, always sure of gliding to a perfect-ten finish. Whereas I feel I'm trying to get this really crap car going, and it just keeps stalling on me. And then other times I feel like my life's a train thundering towards me, and I'm in a car stuck on the crossroads and can't get out. Isn't it great being young!

We came up level with a bunch of twelve-year-olds from Varndean Comp; they were playing with a skipping rope and looked really sweet. Then, as we passed, I realized that they were singing some Eminem song about rape and murder as a skipping rhyme! I raised my eyebrows at Saint, and she chuckled and said, as she peered into a box of Fetherlite to see how many were left, 'Kids today, eh?'

'So what was the message?' I asked her as we came up to her gate. 'About the film.' They never show you films or play you pop records at school without there being a message in it. That kills me. Some trendy teacher'll play 'Zombie Nation' – that trance track with no words. But they haven't bothered to listen to it! Then they'll say, 'That's about Prozac. Now can you tell me, any one of you guys, why Prozac is a symptom rather than a cure?' Sir – hello? It's not about Prozac. It's about dancing.

Saint snorted. 'Said it was a – something. What was it? Oh. "Right of passage."'

I sniggered. 'Sounds dirty!'

'Rite, R-I-T-E. It's like this one important thing that has to happen to you, and then –' Saint made her voice all deep and growly like an American newsreader's '– you are no longer a child.'

'What – losing it?'

'No – you're not meant to lose it in America until you're eighteen. They're all virgins, innit? "True Love Waits" an' all that. Na, it's like when you finally find out what a blow job is, or see a dead body. Something important that you never forget. And you're meant to be about fifteen.'

I thought about this as we stopped outside her gate and I handed her books back. She handed me her fag and I had a crafty drag before treading it out. I don't know about dead bodies, but it's weird that American kids don't have sex until they're, like, grown-ups. I don't think we have rites of passage over here any more; kids are born knowing everything, I think. I don't know whether that's good or bad.

I must have been doing some sort of cheesy frowning thing, because Saint looked at me hard, put her hand on my arm and said, 'Listen. You wanna come in?'

I looked at her house, big and brash and detached – a house that looked you square in the eye and had nothing to hide. No curtains, not even nets, just modern blinds pulled right up revealing the cool yet cosy interior. I could see the TV on and the back of Clio's head, Saint's little sister, as she watched some boy band prancing around swearing that she was the only one for them. Saint had her own portable up in her room; we'd go to the kitchen, grab Diet Cokes and low-fat crisps and – after Saint had said hi to her little sister and made her cry by casually confiding that her latest heart-throb was gay – just kick back upstairs, her sprawling on the bed and me tucked up on the huge window seat. The smell of hair gel and Hard Candy nail varnish, the blur of pop-star posters and kids' TV, the taste of saccharin and salt would lull me into a half-trance like so many times before. GirlWorld: abandon all daily grind and greyness, you who enter here. It was very tempting.

'No, I'm OK.'

Saint laughed. 'Yeah, right.' She opened the gate, stepped inside and stood facing me. 'Well, you need me, call me, OK?'

I didn't even need to answer, just made a two-fingers-down-throat gesture.

She laughed and I turned back to the scenic route to hell.

If I get to the next red car in ten steps, Stella will have come home. Done it. If I can get to the next break in the grass verge in eight, she'll stay.

Screw it!

Stella is my mum. I suppose I should have known she was weird from the start, getting me to call her Stella instead of Mum, but I just thought she was just being friendly. I didn't know she was getting me used to thinking of her as a friend or a sister or whatever so that one day she could just leave home and I wouldn't miss her that much, not like you would someone you called Mum. This is how dumb she is! I couldn't believe it when my eyes filled with tears yet again and I muttered under my breath, 'Oh, Stella, you stupid bitch!'

As I opened the gate, I looked at our house and, though it was big and lush like Saint's, I didn't get the same vibe from it at all. The windows were blank, like eyes dull from a hangover; the front door seemed to frown, sending out vibes which would discourage the casual caller. I'd noticed that, since Stella left, even the Jehovah's Witnesses were giving us a wide berth, and if that doesn't make you feel like a social pariah nothing does. We didn't even seem to get junk mail any more; supermarket special offers narrowed their eyes at our diminished unit and denied us their family-size products, while pizza-delivery flyers got up and walked next door, wondering how on earth they were meant to deliver us a slice of family life when we were such a shadow of our former selves.

I let myself in. You'd think that your mum going would mean the housework started to slide, but it was the opposite with us. The house was spotless, flawless – soulless. Like a beautifully embalmed corpse. Stella had been slapdash, but her domestic shortcomings were part of what had made the house a home. Yellow lilies swooning in a vase, oranges a day too ripe in the dish on the coffee table, the TV always on low in the background – the smell and sound of a household all too human muddling along and doing its best. Now the flowers had been replaced by plants, the fruit stayed in the fridge and the TV was kept mute until there was 'something worth watching' on. We would sit there dutifully watching David Attenborough and, after the credits, off would go the set.

Suddenly we were this whole other family, behaving as though someone were watching us. Saying please and thank you and, 'Oh look, a documentary about molluscs!' Weird.

'A place for everything and everything in its place' – Dad's always liked that saying. He used to get so mad at Stella for not washing the dishes up properly or leaving toothpaste smears in the basin. He used to go around like a demented robot maid, tidying up, shouting about order and efficiency. And, in the end, he tidied himself right out of a marriage, when Stella decided her place was somewhere where a lipsticked coffee cup wasn't a matter for the Crown Prosecution Service.

My brother's blazer was on the banister, so I figured he was up in his room doing his bed act. Every day when Matt gets in, he goes straight upstairs, takes off his uniform and then piles everything in his bedroom that's not fragile or electrical on to the bed. Then, in his underwear, he gets under the covers and under the pile of stuff, trying not to dislodge one thing on to the floor. If one thing falls, he's got to get out of bed, turn around three times clockwise, return the fallen object to where it was and get back in! When he finally makes it, he puts on his Walkman and listens over and over again to this Alan Bennett tape of *The Wind in the Willows* that Stella gave him years ago. This goes on for two hours, till he hears Dad's key in the door. Then he's Mr Normal!

He's only ten. I so, so don't know what to do.

I went into the kitchen and took a Diet Coke from the fridge. I could remember that only a couple of years ago I'd really looked down on people who drank diet softies – it seemed so weird and over-cautious, like wearing your seat belt in the back seat, or actually watching the stewardess pointing out where the emergency exits were. Then suddenly you're fifteen and apparently every girl in your class is studying to become a supermodel, even the ones that say they want to be lawyers or war correspondents, and the exact calorific content of everything, from sugar-free gum to a whole roasted pig, is common knowledge in a way that times tables will never be. When teachers complain that they can't get girls interested in maths, it's just so obvious what they should do: 'Kate has ingested 200 calories every day for a week, while Naomi has taken in 750. If Kate brings up her breakfast twice but eats a bag of Cheesy Wotsits midweek and Naomi has a vodka and slimline on Monday night, what will be the difference in their respective weight losses?' Substitute fruit and nut for fractions, and make the pie charts about real pies, and you'll have straight As all round.

Even if you're really thin, you've got to be on a diet at my school. It's considered babyish to treat food as a source of pleasure – quite rude and crude somehow. What's meant to be normal is treating food like a cross between a time bomb that's about to explode and an outlandishly time-consuming indulgence that you're far too busy to bother with. To hear the girls in my class talk, you'd think there was a law stating, on pain of death if transgressed, that every morsel which passes people's lips in the twenty-first century has to be personally stalked, trapped, butchered and prepared by the individual who's going to eat it. They go into an anti-feeding frenzy: 'Ohmigosh, I've got to be at my Suzuki violin class by five – I haven't got time to eat!' You wouldn't think there were sandwich shops and burger bars. To hear them talk, you'd think they live on air. And then of course they go home and lock themselves in the bathroom and eat a fun-size bag of Snickers. Which is then promptly brought back up in a rather less fun-size form, to the thundering accompaniment of every tap turned on full.

I've never been able to get into the bulimia thing, which makes me so much not one of the in-crowd. I think it's probably because I've got quite a well-developed sense of humour, and if you think about it logically the idea that vomiting is the thing which decides whether you're cool or not is hilarious. It's like thinking that messing yourself is cool. Also, because Stella wasn't ever a conventional mother, and was always buzzing about working or doing her voluntary thing or drinking blue cocktails with her friends in hotel bars, we hardly ever ate together as a family. Now I know that this is meant to be a bad thing, and that my generation are all in danger of becoming serial killers because we don't get meat and two veg slap bang on the dot of seven every night all sitting up straight around the table with Dad carving and Mum looking on admiringly. But from what I've seen and heard at school, it's the girls who come from this sort of set-up who tend to go in big-time for bulimia. If you grow up having to eat when your parents say so, even when you're not hungry, it's bound to become a control issue later on. Stands to reason.

Dad would've liked us to be like that though. 'They'll eat when they're hungry, Nathan!' Stella had yelled so many times. 'They're not livestock, they're bloody individuals! You're not going to milk them or collect their eggs! Do you see either of them wasting away?' Since she'd been gone he'd tried to do the old-fashioned family Sunday lunch thing a couple of times, but the atmosphere had been so sad, in both meanings of the word, that he'd given up.

I know I should have felt sorry for Dad, but I couldn't. Because at the back of my mind I had this horrible nagging suspicion, which was so weird I hadn't even told Saint. No matter how much I told myself to look at the evidence – that he'd been madly in love with Stella, that he'd never have kept on with the nagging if he'd had a clue that it would drive her out, that he'd been left beached and bleached-out by her departure – I kept coming up with the same surreal conclusion.

Which was that Dad was actually secretly pleased she was gone. Because at last he had an excuse to be as miserable, as downbeat, as pessimistic as he'd always wanted to be. He'd done his best to be sad when Stella was there, but her bouncy, almost manic cheerfulness always swooped down and rescued him from the quicksand at the last minute. Now he could wallow as luxuriously as he wanted; now no one could tell him that he should cheer up because it might never happen again. Because it had happened, once and for all, and now he really did have something to whine about.

Downstairs I heard a key in the door. He was home. Whatever home means.

2

I stood stock-still by my open bedroom door, listening to Dad listen to the absence of Stella. That was always the worst bit, the moment you opened the door and forgot for a minute she wasn't there. The silence was deafening.

I know it sounds a bit weird, but if Stella hadn't been such a noisy bitch I don't think we'd miss her quite as much. But we were so used to coming home from school and hearing the TV blaring Jerry or Trisha from the living room, switched on by Stella in an idle moment and then abandoned, the radio blasting dance music from the kitchen – Stella loved the local station, Juice FM, despite the fact that they only seem to have five records and three of them are by Anastacia. Competing with it all would be the roar of her state-of-the-art blender as it whizzed up yet another undrinkable health drink, while Stella herself could be heard shrieking on the phone upstairs to one of her numerous blonde girlfriends.

I'm blonde, Matt's blond, Dad's blond – Stella doesn't seem to know any brunettes. Dad used to say half-jokingly that she was such a control freak that she even had to make the state of blondness, which is usually thought to be something special, into a humdrum backdrop for her own glossy darkness, and I think on balance he probably had something. I mean, we're talking about a woman so shallow and vain that she used to lie about her star sign; didn't like being an

Aries, said it sounded nasty, so pretended she was a Leo. Leading to the ridiculous situation of her having two birthdays, like the Queen; one for the family in April, one for the outside world in August. But expected presents from me, Matt and Dad for both of course!

I'd always found the racket comforting, but Dad hated it. In his tidy mind, where there was a place for everything and everything in its place, random noise offended him as much as a vase of blowsy flowers dropping petals or a pair of muddy shoes abandoned on the stairs. He'd go through the house turning stuff off, and then go and stand glowering at Stella as she shrieked away on the blower, until she got the message and hung up. I guess he must have done it once too often, because one day he came home from work and the house was silent apart from the sound of Matt and me crying over a piece of paper we'd found on the kitchen table. She'd gone.

I went downstairs; Dad was hanging up his coat. I swear as he turned round he was smiling – not in a normal smiley way, but in a sort of 'bittersweet' way. That had always been one of his favourite words, bittersweet, and I couldn't help thinking that part of the reason he used it so much was because it always annoyed the hell out of Stella. 'Look, Nathan, things are either nice or they're nasty. They can't be both,' she'd snarl. I was always inclined to agree with her.

When he saw me he stopped smiling. He came over and kissed me on top of the head. 'Kimmy. How's it going?'

'Fine.' I just knew he had something to tell me. And I

also knew that whatever it was wasn't going to make me jump in the air and shout, 'Whoop-de-doo!'

'Come and talk to me while I get supper on.' Supper. Stella stubbornly called it 'tea', having once been working class and finding supper too up itself. Of course this led to numerous avoidable misunderstandings, when she invited my schoolmates to tea and found that they were there at four o'clock expecting cake and dinky sandwiches with the crusts cut off instead of sticking around till seven and eating with us. And of course at four she wouldn't be home. She'd breeze in at six and refuse to understand why my 'stuck-up little chum' had gone home. Saint was the only one who got it – who got Stella generally; I would often catch them sneaking a quick fag in the kitchen early in the morning after she'd slept over. They'd laugh at me fondly but condescendingly when I stumbled in, still bleary from sleep in my Snoopy nightshirt, and staggered round opening all the windows to let the smoke out.

'Oh, Kim!' Stella would squeal. 'Spare us the great outdoors, darling! It's Arctic out there!

'Chill, Kimbo,' Saint would tut-tut. 'It's too early to get down with the elements.'

'It wouldn't hurt you to be a bit more like Zoe, sweetheart,' Stella would say when I was winding myself up over GCSEs and stuff. 'Don't let these things get on top of you. Education's about a lot more than passing exams.'

'You're not much like your mum, are you?' Saint would say glumly when I'd gone over to study at her house and she suggested we break for half an hour's malicious texting. 'She's always up for it.'

So up for it, in fact, that she'd run off with a twenty-eight-year-old whose house she was decorating in Kemp Town. Only now they'd hoofed it to his other house. In the Bahamas. He'd made millions from the Internet.

'Jammy!' said Saint when she found out. 'Think we can go out and stay with her?' She'd had the grace to look guilty when she saw the look on my face, but it was definitely the closest I ever came to gouging her eyes out and shoving them up her nostrils.

I followed Dad into the kitchen and sat down at the table. He'd always had a bee in his bonnet about the kitchen and tried to make it 'the heart of the home', like in Europe. He bought a big rustic table and on the shelves there were jars with French words on and lots of glazed pottery mugs hanging up. But to Stella there was one thing missing – a telly! That was just like her. Like the time we went on safari in Kenya and she moaned because there weren't any shops. She said this while our jeep was about three yards away from a family of elephants taking a dust bath! Elephants, and she's going on about running out of facial scrub! So lots of nights Dad had his supper in the kitchen, and Stella had her tea in the front room watching *EastEnders*. We'd want to join her, but the thought of our dad sitting there eating his pasta alone in this room he'd tried to make so cosy, among the French jars and friendly mugs, was just too tragic.

'Shall I do something?' I asked him now. He was standing at the sink, filling a big saucepan with water.

'No, babe, it's OK.' He put it on the cooker and came to sit down across the table from me. 'Kimmy. You like school, don't you?'

'It's OK.' What a weird question. Where was this going?

'How would you feel about – if you had to change schools. Go to school somewhere else.'

For one wild minute I thought he was going to send me to the Bahamas. I had this vision of myself, barefoot and golden brown and wearing a blue pinafore, walking along a silver beach to school with a beautiful boy who looked like a young Lenny Kravitz. 'You mean in the Bahamas?'

He looked annoyed. 'No, not in the Bahamas! Believe it or not, not all roads lead to your mother. Here. In Brighton.'

'But why?' I wasn't upset, just curious.

He sighed deeply, if somewhat theatrically. 'Money, Kim. I'm afraid I just can't afford to keep you at the High any longer. Without two incomes coming in.'

Come on! I couldn't believe Stella's money was either here or there; she only decorated about one house every six months and spent most of her earnings on clothes and cocktails, from what I'd seen. 'So what do you want me to do?'

'Sweetheart, I'm afraid you're going to have to leave the High and go to Ravendene Comp.'

'Ravendene . . .'

Every city's got a school like Ravendene; the source and inspiration for 5,000 urban myths and horror stories. The pupils – the Ravers – were undoubtedly feared, allegedly loathed and secretly envied by the remainder of the adolescent population of Brighton. All the girls were on the Pill at eleven; all the boys skilled thieves and fraudsters by the age of twelve.

And oh, their beauty and grace! No one I knew personally actually knew a Raver. In Preston Park? Come on! But I'd seen a few from afar and they looked like they'd come from some Planet Melting Pot where the Italians took care of the skin, the Swedes saw to the height, and the Caribbeans had run the infant dancing classes.

The Ravers it was, past and present, who had caused West Street on a Friday and Saturday night – from dusk till dawn, from the clock tower at the top to the very edge of the sea – to be known by the locals, police included, as 'Little Beirut', and as such totally out of bounds to nice girls like me. And now my own father was planning to drop me into the belly of the beast.

'. . . a reputation, and I wouldn't normally consider it, but they've just got this new head, from a private girls' school no less, and she's determined to put it into turnaround,' he was saying. He was staring me hard in the face. Staring me down, I suddenly thought. Waiting for me to cry. Waiting for me to say, 'Please, please, don't make me go!' Waiting for me to blame Stella. Waiting for me to write her a hateful letter saying it was all her fault. Waiting for the guilt-ridden cheque inside the registered letter with the Bahamian stamp. Well, he'd wait a long time.

19

I stared back and smiled. He couldn't hide his shock. 'That's great, Dad. When do I start?'

'You can't leave. You can't!' Saint slammed herself down on her bed. She banged her fists on the duvet and actually kicked her heels. I couldn't help smiling. You could tell she still had two parents at home; she was such a kid.

I sat down beside her and put my hand on her back. 'Zo –'

'Don't CALL me that!' She jumped up on to her knees and glared at me. 'See? It's already happening –'

'It's your name –'

'But it's not ME, Kim! It's a bloody white girl's name! Not ME! Only YOU know ME! And now you're going away from me!'

'I'm not going anywhere.' I grabbed at her hand. She looked about twelve, with tears on her lips. 'I'll still live two streets away. We'll see each other every night, and nothing will have changed –'

'God, will you listen to yourself! You're talking like a parent who's about to walk out! The same LIES!'

I took my hand away. This remark was somewhat lacking in tact and sensitivity, to say the least. 'Well, if you weren't acting like such a silly little kid, I might not be acting like a parent.'

'Go on then!' She came off the bed like a gymnast, and made a perfect landing on my feelings. 'Piss off, like your mum did!'

I ran down the stairs, and as I grabbed my schoolbag

from the coat rack I could hear Saint banging on an upstairs door. There was a click, a thump and a wail, so I figured it had been Clio's bedroom.

I'm better off without her, I told myself as I walked home, my legs wobbly and my breathing rapid. Who wants a best friend who thinks it's perfectly OK to take out her temper on her eleven-year-old sister? She's just a bully.

And there wouldn't be any of them where I was going of course. Amongst the Ravers of Ravendene Comp, I would at last find a best friend worthy of me. If I lived past registration.

3

From the first time I ever saw Sugar – Maria Sweet – sitting on that wall in the schoolyard, she seemed to me to be moving in slow motion, which is strange because she wasn't in any way sluggish or even sexily languid. Looking back, I can see that she tended to sit stock-still and then, her mind made up, dart suddenly and somewhat clumsily in pursuit of whatever chosen aim or target took her fancy, for good or ill. She was tall, long-limbed, but had exceptionally small feet, which gave her a teetering walk, even in flat school shoes. It was something to do with the length of her eyes, the slowness of her smile and the swoosh of her lovely, almost waist-length long hair, as dark as hair can be without being black, which gave the impression of soft-focus, shimmering slo-mo.

She certainly stood out. As I hung around in the playground – what an innocent, childlike word to describe such an arena of torment! – trying not to look as if my uniform (scarlet sweater, black skirt/trousers – not half bad if legend didn't have it that the Ravers uniform was chosen so the top half wouldn't show the bloodstains and the bottom wouldn't show the dirt as none of their mums had washing machines) was new, I couldn't help thinking that the girl sitting smoking ostentatiously on the wall, surrounded by acolytes, had been the main beneficiary of the fabled Italian skin and Swedish height. (You could tell by her arm movements and the way she swayed as she spoke that she was a good dancer too.) For the rest, the allegedly beauteous Raver girls seemed only slightly better looking than my old gang at the High, and that only because they wore more make-up and had proper haircuts. And they were so much shorter, which was cheering. The girls at the High had been giants, but here I could pass for normal . . .

Then the boys arrived.

A swarming, seething mass of testosterone, a symphony of savagery in scarlet and black. I gasped at the sight of so many teenage boys at once. They were tall and short, fat and thin, pale and swarthy, but they all seemed to move with a feral, swerving grace, looking out from under lowered eyelids at their surroundings as though seeing them for the first time yet trying to hide the fact, like thieves casing a jackable joint. They looked, above all, guilty as hell.

Then the pack faded into soft-focus backdrop and all I could see was The One. He was every teenage dream rebel cliché made flesh and made new. His dark, silky quiff, his razor-sharp cheekbones, his hooded eyes, his mouth like the very first kiss God created. His tall and slender state of grace. Suddenly, all at once, every vile sex-ed lesson made perfect sense. It made perfect sense too when he swerved in my direction. I was in an actual swoon, which is probably a good thing, because I'm sure what happened next would have been even more humiliating if I'd been fully conscious.

Not breaking his stride, not raising his eyes, The One put his right hand lightly on my left breast – ohmigod, with a real actual NIPPLE sticking out! – squeezed twice in rapid succession and husked, 'Beep beep!'

His cronies fell about, but they all kept moving. I stood there, my face rapidly turning as red as my sweater – all the better, please, for me to disappear. I think I would have turned and walked out forever, just kept walking until I turned sixteen and could get a job in a far county – Dorset perhaps? – where the story of my shaming might not have spread, had not the beautiful smoking girl uttered a deafening cry of such guttural rage that I felt a mad instinctive impulse to throw myself in front of my molester and protect him.

She was off that wall as if pitched from it by an unseen hand, teetering slightly on her tiny feet, strutting rapidly with the coming-atcha single-mindedness unfamiliar in these isles until the import of the American catfight shows.

The One stopped in his tracks and swore under his breath. In a very, very resigned way. In fact, it sounded almost like a prayer. But it didn't help, as her long arm whiplashed out, caught him by the collar and swung him round to face her.

'What did I say, Jesus?' she hissed at him. She shook him hard. 'Jesus? What did I say to you last Sunday afternoon, by the bins at Burger King?'

He mumbled something.

'What, Jesus? Bit louder. I don't think Blondie here heard you.'

'Sorry,' he mumbled, raising his eyes briefly to mine. They were muddy and dull and without that vital spark

24

that signals intelligence, no matter how unschooled – not so much the windows to his soul as the windows to a nasty old shed with woodlice in and dirty old torn-out pages from a porn magazine. I breathed a sigh of relief. I needn't love him after all.

'Thassit!' she cried triumphantly. She had a strange voice; husky, but occasionally collapsing to a squeak, like a boy whose voice has almost but not quite broken. Her accent was working-class Brighton, which I can only describe as cockney without the cockiness. She swung the boy – no longer The One! – round once for good measure and let him go, observing with a smile of satisfaction his subsequent congress with a vicious-looking brick wall. 'You are SO on parole!'

As the boy stumbled away with a single backward glance of fear, mingled with what could only be respect, the girl turned to me. Her face fell as she looked at my chest. 'Bloody hell, Blondie. You can't really blame the sad act. Look at 'em! You trying to tell which way the wind's blowing or what?'

I looked down. It was my nipples; having discovered the power of speech, they wouldn't shut up. I felt the blood streaming back into my face and looked at the ground. Or where the ground would have been without these huge scarlet breasts, tipped by what appeared to be pointing fingers, in the way.

But the girl laughed and threw her arm around me. She smelt of vanilla and chips. 'Come on. You're the new girl, you're in my class. You come and sit by me.'

'Thank you,' I managed to mutter as we followed the sound of the bell. 'I could use a friend.'

'Oh, I'm not your friend.' My saviour looked surprised. 'It's just that this is MY school. I'm Maria Sweet – Sugar. If you get bullied, it'll be when I say so. Not when my sodding brother acts like a dog.' She looked at my chest and nodded in approval. 'That's more like it. Suddenly you don't look so up for it.' She shot me a brilliant smile and pulled me into the classroom. 'Was it something I said?'

For two weeks Maria Sweet didn't speak to me. (Thankfully her brother, the singularly inappropriately named Jesus, was a year above us, and kept a respectful distance in the playground.) I didn't mind an awful lot; I felt safe, with some sort of invisible bubble of protection around me. Ravendene wasn't anything like as bad as urban myth would have it, but this might have been because the new head, Mrs Rockminster, was still an unknown quantity, and the fact that she had given up a good job at a posh school to come here left the Ravers feeling rather confused and first-footed.

Then Sugar was off sick with some throat thing for a month and when she came back her power, so evident before, had waned. Girls had compared notes and found her signature false. Popular girls usually gain and keep their power by the oldest trick in the book, divide and rule, and a period of extended absence is the quickest way to see a teenage empire crumble.

Not being familiar with the intricacy of Sugar Sweet's

empire, I wasn't part of the drama that slowly unfolded during break and lunchtime, and so was left standing on the sidelines, trying to ignore the hopeful smiles of the lividly freckled swot who was the only girl in the class Sugar hadn't even bothered to tell one lie about. I wasn't interested in having a friend anyway, I told myself on the long, lonely walk home each day – and certainly not that crazed diva Zoe Clements. I only walked past her house so much, even though it was out of my way, because I was trying to go the long way home in order to walk off some weight. I only called her mobile from public phones at night in order to annoy her. Not to listen to her VOICE or anything dumb like that. Her loud, bossy, always-right voice. Which was now for some reason a subdued, docile, what-did-I-do-wrong voice. Especially when she said, 'Kim? Kimbo? Is that you? Please, Kimbo. Come back.' But she never said sorry for being such a bitch. So she could just wait, and I would wait too, patiently, until Saint discovered the magic word.

Sugar cornered me in the playground at break on her third day back. 'I can't stick this much longer. You wanna go around?'

'Around where?'

She rolled her eyes and spoke slowly, as if to an idiot. 'Around with me. Hang. Have a laugh. Whatever.'

'Yeah.' I fought a desire to punch the air. 'OK. Whatever.'

'Come back with me after school then. Call home on your mobey and leave a message.'

'I don't have a mobile.'

She peered at me suspiciously, as if suspecting herself to be the victim of some elaborate practical joke, then saw I was for real and sighed deeply, shaking her head. I saw the slo-mo thing again. She dug in her bag, pressed some buttons and handed me a lurid leopard-print-covered mobile. PORN STAR, said the screen.

I dialled our number and the BT lady said her piece, prompting mine. 'Dad, I'm going to my friend's house after school today. I'll be back around seven –'

Sugar shook her head and held up both her hands, fingers spread. 'Ten, I mean. Bye!' I gave the phone back to her, staring at her in alarm. How suggestible was I! 'I can't stay out till ten on a school night!'

'Why, you gonna turn into a pumpkin-head?' She put her phone away and took out a mirror and lipstick. 'Why d'you tell your dad, not your mum? She dead?'

'She left home six months ago.'

She stared at me, her mouth open. 'What, with a bloke?'

'Yeah. They live in the Bahamas.'

'Your dad knock her around?'

'No. He tried to make the kitchen the heart of the household.'

She gave me A Look. 'What, he knocked down the living-room wall without asking her?'

'He bought big jars with French words on.'

She looked again, then laughed. She grabbed my arm. 'Come on, let's go.'

'But we've got chemistry . . .'

'Ooh, darling, never knew you cared!' She made a kissing noise at me, then dragged me towards the school gates. 'The day they show us how to make a gram of whizz, that's when I'll get interested in chemistry . . .

'Come on, let's go down the pier. I saw Zoë Ball there last week with the baby! She's dead cool, gave me a big smile. And I saw that bloke, the fit one off the telly with the wonky eye – he stared really hard at me, least his good eye did! If I see him again, I'm going to lie about my age, pull him and sell my story to the papers. Majestic!'

All roads in Brighton lead to the pier; not the sad, beautiful, ruined West Pier but the cheap, cheerful, thriving Palace Pier. No matter how many times I go there – a lot less than you'd think, because when you live in a place it sort of disappears for you, and you don't do the things that tourists do – I'm always excited as I step on. The blare of the music, the smell of onions, cheeseburgers and candyfloss, the sight of the sea through the boards makes me feel dizzy, but in a good way, like something brilliant's about to happen. But being there with Maria Sweet made it something else. She belonged there; she was that tough, that loud, that all-consuming.

'When I was a kid I used to have nightmares about this pier collapsing too,' she said as we stopped by the first set of sheltered seats for her to fire up a Marlboro Light. 'I used to think of all the horses on the merry-go-round, all fallen apart, just lying there at the bottom of the sea – all their weird grinning faces with them big teeth showing? Jesus!' She shuddered. 'It still turns me over just thinking about it! When we get up the end, right, I always close my eyes and you'll have to guide me past it.' We walked on. 'I used to mix up nightmare with merry-go-round, my mum says, and I'd wake up in the night screaming about the night-merry!' She laughed. 'Sad, innit?'

'I used to dream that I was trying to write on a black-board,' I said, 'but where there should have been chalk, there was just my fingers, and they were bleeding, and I was trying to write my name on the board without anyone noticing it wasn't chalk in case I got told off and made to write an extra essay, because I knew that I'd have to write with my bleeding stumps . . .' I trailed off as she stopped and stared at me. 'What?'

'Jeez. Just scary, that's all.'

We got to the Pleasuredome, the first of two big covered arcades. 'You got money?' Sugar asked me.

'About a tenner.'

'I got . . .' She scratched in her pocket. 'I got ten too. Come on, let's get gaming.'

It sounds weird, but that's when it started – what I felt for Sugar. It was the flashing lights, and the noise of the machines, and the loud, loud music, all seeming to refract and contract around her, her eyes widening, her hair swooshing, her slow smile shining. She seemed an actual part of the place – all fun, all joy, all shimmery skittering energy. So far away from the stillness and sadness of my house, which was no longer a home or anything corny and wonderful like that, so different from me and my ceaseless, wearisome responsibility, anxiety and moderation. I was fifteen, and I was already an old woman!

I looked at her, bent in childlike concentration over the Goldrush machine, not a care in the world, and I wanted to be like her.

And when I woke up in the morning, I wanted her. Something must have happened in my dreams. But I'm getting ahead of myself here.

'Frig it!' Sugar was holding on to the machine and kicking it hard. A wail went up from it. She grabbed my hand. 'It's wired! Come on, do one before they chuck us off!'

We stumbled giggling further into the Pleasuredome, Sugar pulling me behind her as she moved with her weird, cute, teetering run. I became aware of the song they were playing – that old Italian handbag house hit, sung by one of those girls whose name you will never remember but whose voice you will never forget, and it stuck in my mind because the first words I was aware of, in that girl's lovely aching voice, were, 'Sugar, you make my soul complete . . . rapture tastes so sweet.' My giggling turned to laughter, really carefree loud laughter, the first since Stella left, and without asking why or even turning to look at me Sugar did the same. I suddenly felt so magnificently, incandescently happy that I felt I could fly, if the need arose, right off the side of the pier, swooping towards the ruined beauty of the

West Pier. I could heal it with my big shiny happiness, which I visualized for some reason as masses of hundreds and thousands, falling from me like fairy dust.

Sugar stopped, still laughing, leaning against a huge screen. 'You play fight games?'

'Yeah!' I had a few times, with Saint, because OF COURSE the psycho bitch from hell liked beat-'em-ups, but I wasn't very good

'Get on then.' She gestured to the seats in front of it, and put two pound coins into a slot.

It was Tekken; I'd played this one before. As the characters came up, Sugar exclaimed gleefully, 'Jeez, you look just like Nina!' There was a slight physical resemblance between myself and the Silent Assassin, but it stopped there; Saint had commented on it witheringly – 'Ain't it a shame, Kimbo, that you can't do the Spiral Explosion or the Geyser Cannon Combo? Or even the Paper Bag Fight-Way-Out-Of?' Well, the cow could eat dirt now; I was on the pier with SUGAR SWEET!

She pressed the button to make me Nina. 'And I'll be Jun, cos she looks like me.' She did too, even though Jun was nominally Japanese; long, sloe eyes, golden skin, leaping dark hair.

'She's beautiful,' I heard a voice say softly, and I realized it was mine.

Sugar didn't hear me; she was crouched excitedly over her dashboard. 'Fight!'

I think I realized then that I was never going to escape my extreme moderation when I couldn't bring myself to hurt Sugar. Jun, rather. Suprisingly, Sugar was rubbish at the game too – she didn't approach it logically like Zoe, who would study the buttons and moves for a good five minutes before putting her money in, oblivious to the exasperated sighs of the other people waiting to play.

Once, when some big bruiser had been sighing too loudly to allow her to concentrate on her studies, she turned to him and said sweetly, 'Mate, do you have a problem? Apart from the fact that your arse and your face seem to have traded places?' Then she kissed him full on the lips, so fast you could hardly believe it had happened. She was just so sure of herself, so pretty, that the bruiser and his mates, after a second's shocked silence, burst out laughing. They hung around cheering her on for the whole three games we played – the final one the kissed fool even paid for! – and of course Muggins here was decimated, with all that negative energy coming my way. That's Saint all over; she doesn't want friends, she wants fan clubs.

Got to stop thinking about Saint! Sugar could make mincemeat of her.

However, she sucked at Tekken. It was a fiasco! She made no attempt to maximize the firepower of Jun's specialities – Funeral Palm, Demon Slayer or even Dragon Wheel Vacuum Spin Kick – but instead just banged the buttons repeatedly with the heel of her hand! Even I could make Nina do her Ray Hands move. I'm not just upping myself here, but I really could have beat her.

Except . . . I couldn't beat her up. I couldn't hurt her.

Even when she was only nine inches high and going incognito as Jun Kazama, Ecological Fighter.

Nina's Ray Hands stayed still and her Creep Rush was rooted to the spot as Jun, through sheer brute force, claimed a perfect KO time and time again, even as she performed her pointless repertoire of somersaults, spins and running in the opposite direction to her enemy. Sugar, bless her, didn't notice that I was letting her win, probably because she was totally clueless. 'Yeah!' she exclaimed after the third match. 'Friggin' A!' She threw her arms around me. They were very, very long. I could run, but I couldn't hide from those long arms. 'Loser buys the waffles, Kiz!'

Kiz? I almost objected, but then it struck me that I liked it, and that I wanted to BE the sort of person who would be called Kiz. Kiz was a tough girl, a worthy sidekick for Sugar Sweet – not the Kimmy of her doting dad or the condescended-to Kimbo-the-Bimbo of the ever-superior Saint Clements, just because I was blonde with big tits.

And it sounded like *Kiss*. And it was Sugar's own, her very own name for me . . .

I bought the waffles, and wiped chocolate off her chin. Then we went back to her place. It was the best day of my life.

34

4

As we rode up the hill to the Ravendene Estate, in the front seat on top of the bus, I felt suddenly shy. I was crap at going to people's houses, always had been; I laughed at the wrong moments and frowned when a joke had been cracked. Because of my weird over-conscientiousness, I seemed unable to get along with both my contemporaries – who thought I was boring – and their parents, who thought I was a snob. Saint, with her sophistication and self-possession, was envied by kids and invariably charmed their parents, even though she smoked and shagged like a sailor on shore leave. But when you're shy, you just seem stuck-up. Or worse: Saint once told me, between gasps of laughter, that her mother thought I was 'on drugs', merely because I was so quiet. And she'd said, 'Give me a break, Mum! Kimbo takes two Junior Disprin, she thinks she's walking on the wild side!"

But the minute I walked into the Sweet house – my first council house! I registered – I knew it was going to be just fine. There was a wail, a whoosh and a shriek; 'AH-VEY?! That you? Help me!

We rushed into the kitchen; there was a chip pan on fire, and Sugar's mum, Suzy, a frail, red-headed woman, was throwing cupfuls of water on it.

'DON'T DO THAT!' I yelled. I pushed Sugar out of the way, grabbed a tea towel, soaked it under the cold tap and boldly thrust it on to the pan. There was a final spiteful burst and then a sizzle, and the flames subsided.

The red-headed lady looked at me gratefully and gave me the sweetest smile. Her teeth looked as though a tiny car had gone joyriding in her mouth. 'Ooh! I always KNOW that's what you do, but I panic! And then I forget . . .'

'There are more fires in East Brighton than in any other zone of the city,' I heard myself saying. 'Therefore the council have pledged to send a safety officer to each household by next year, to explain the many benefits of smoke alarms.' I caught Sugar and her mother exchanging amazed glances; dear God, why was I such a freak? Stella hadn't liked the council one bit, and was actually once officially cautioned by the police for making nuisance phone calls to the lady leader, who soon after resigned to have a nervous breakdown. It's no wonder I'm so weird.

Sugar sat down with a snigger at the kitchen table. It wasn't even a distant relation of ours; it was tiny, topped with peeling Formica. The sort of thing Stella could sell, in better condition, to 'some poor sucker' as 'ironic'. 'White-trash chic,' she called it. I'd always hated that phrase. It meant working class, obviously, so not only was it incredibly rude, but it would also appear to go directly against Stella's alleged working-class sympathies! No wonder I'm confused. I couldn't believe it when Saint started saying it too. How would she feel about working-class blacks being called black trash? ('Lighten up, Kimbo!' she laughed with Stella in the kitchen when I made this point. 'We're just messin' wit' you!')

'Mum, make us a sarnie! And one for Kiz, she's staying for a bit.'

'Ooh . . . I've got corned beef, sandwich spread, wafer-thin turkey . . . '

'Got any crisps?'

'Salt and vin?'

'We'll have a crisp sandwich, twice, and Tango.' She stood up. 'We'll be in my bedroom.'

'OK, love.' Mrs Sweet smiled absently, turning to her task.

Leaving the kitchen, our joyous passage was blocked by two of the ugliest kids I swear I've ever seen in my life. About eight years old, livid red hair, freckles that, if you tried to join them up with a pen, would make you think they were in the SAS, wearing camouflage. And the colour of their skin – which made the freckles seem a blessing – the nastiest skin tone I've ever seen, like the paint old people would do their hallways in, called something like 'Apple White'. I swear they had a green tinge.

And there were two of them! Identical! It was one of those moments when you totally wonder what God was playing at. Like making a giraffe's neck so long that it finds it hard to find suitable foliage, or making a zebra so starkly black and white that it can't blend in and hide from preda-tors anywhere but on a zebra crossing. Like He just got to the end of a long day and thought, 'Sod it, I've created the dolphin and the golden Labrador today – I've done my bit, now no more Mr Nice Guy!'

The ugly kids stared at us. 'Who's she?' said one of the freaks, pointing.

'She's my new sister,' whispered Sugar urgently. 'Mum saw her picture in the *Argus*, up for adoption, and rung up the Social and asked if she could swap two ugly little ratbags for one pretty daughter, my age, for company. If I was you, I'd go and pack your Barbies in your bumbags. They'll be here to take you to the Home any minute.'

They wailed as one – 'MUUUUM!' – and pushed past us, heading for the kitchen.

Sugar smirked, and indicated the way with a twist of her lovely head. 'Me and JJ take after our dad, you might have sussed. THEY don't.'

As we walked up the stairs, I remembered something: 'Who's Ah-Vey?'

'That's me.' We reached the landing. 'I'm Ave-Maria. JJ, he's Jesus-Joseph. And you'll never guess what the gruesome twosome are called –' She pushed a door open.

I relaxed; I was in GirlWorld. No matter what the difference in background, GirlWorld makes daydreaming, water-treading sisters of us all. The posters of boys, torn from magazines, on the walls, the fruity cosmetics on the dressing table, the tiny tops from Morgan and Kookaï strewn across the floor, the CDs out of their boxes, snatched off in the heat of the moment of having to hear THAT SONG, RIGHT NOW. Until after one and a half minutes you remembered the one you REALLY wanted to hear.

'No, what?'

She indicated the bed. I sat down. 'Get this. They're

called She-Ra – and Evil-Lyn!' She was sorting through CDs; she held up a party-coloured box containing the sort of dance-tune compilation that I had often yearned over in Virgin but then turned my treacherous back on, because I am – was – a High girl, and High girls listen to Dido and Radiohead and hardcore rap about how many drive-by shootings you've pulled and how many bitches you've slapped, as we chew our pens over our algebra homework, because we're, like, so intelligent or something that we know they're only 'ironic' shootings and slappings.

'Come on – you're joking!'

'No, honest. My dad named them, before he did a runner. Thought it was funny. He'd already gone off with some other woman, but she threw him out and he came back. Nine months later, Skanky and Manky arrive. Mum's desperate to keep him, so she says he can name the brats, so long as they've got two names, like me and Jay. Anyway, we don't talk about it. They're Shera and Evelyn to everybody else.' She pushed a button and the sound of Stardust doing 'Music Sounds Better With You' filled the room. I'd never gone for it before, found it cheesy beyond the call of duty and beauty, but suddenly it made sense.

The door opened; first a tray came round it, bearing sandwiches and softies, then Mrs Sweet's hopeful, foolish face. ''Scuse me –'

'Put it there, Mum.' Sugar indicated the pouffe in front of the dressing table, frowning as if she was a Michelin critic finding fault with the service.

'Jay been back?'

'He was, but he went . . . out.'

'I'll bet he did!' Sugar glared at her mother. 'We'll talk about it later.'

'Yes, love,' replied Mrs Sweet with a tranquil semi-smile. Amazingly, out of the blue, I suddenly had this flash that she found Sugar silly, and was trying to hide the fact for fear of hurting her feelings. The door closed quietly after her.

Sugar sighed heavily, stood up and pressed a button on her CD player – 'Girls Like Us' by the B-15 Project. 'That brother of mine. Don't even go there.'

'What? Sorry, you don't have to say –'

She responded immediately. 'He's out jacking, innee? Breaking, entering, lifting – you name it. I wouldn't mind, but he's crap. It's a joke. Either he cuts himself on the window on the way in, or he goes A over T on the way out. Whatever, he screws up. The police come round with him, yet again, LAUGHING at us. And Shoshanna Murphy, in Jay's class, her dad's always the copper that grabs him! He's making this family a laughing stock –' She stood in front of the full-length mirror on the door of her wardrobe, scowling, then leaning forward to check out the suggestion of a blemish on her chin. 'Frig it! I'm not asking him to do a bank robbery. All I ask is for him to be able to jack a pair of trainers without being marched home by the collar. The Sweets used to have respect round here . . .'

She spun around and flung herself down on the bed next to me – her hair was so long, and had so much body, that I swear it took a good five seconds to resettle around her face and shoulders. I really should have hated her, like ordinary girls are meant to with gorgeous ones – though in my limited experience, female bitchiness isn't as common as boys would like it to be (with the exception of that filthy-tempered mentalist Zoe Clements of course). For some reason, boys – and men – find the idea of women being nasty to each other really attractive, don't they?

'So! You done it then? Go on, let's have all the gory details!'

She broke into my thoughts.

'What,' I said, playing for time, but not insulting her by putting the question mark on the end. Of course we both knew what she was talking about.

'You have, haven't you?' She laughed silently like a cartoon creature, all her teeth showing. 'I knew you had! Everyone always says you High girls are right slappers!'

'Well, that's funny, cos everyone else says it about you lot too!' I knew straight away that if I didn't diss her back, I wouldn't be coming back for a repeat performance. 'What's a Raver girl's idea of a real classy romance? – having him stop the car first!'

'Bitch!' She caught me by the wrists and knocked me backwards on the bed. Her hands were thin and strong. 'What's a High girl do if she really likes you? – lets you be first in the queue, and come back for seconds!'

'Raver girls don't believe in queuing though, do they?' I laughed up at her. 'It's first come, first served, with you. All you can eat for the price of a Bacardi Breezer!'

She didn't miss a beat, just squeezed my wrists hard for

a second. 'Yeah, but the last boy I went out with, he accused me of being an expensive date because YOU did it for half a bag of Monster Munch!'

I was just about to accuse her of putting out for a lick of a Cheestrings wrapper – nice to know my expensive education wasn't wasted, no? – when the door opened wide and JJ's lovely dumb face leered at us. 'Having fun, girls?'

Maria jumped up and smoothed her skirt down. 'Where you been?'

'Out.' He sat down on the pouffe and looked at himself in the mirror. Then he tilted it and sat back, smirking. 'Nice knickers, Kizza. Pink. Or you just pleased to see me?'

Maria pulled me up to a sitting position with one hand and swatted him round the head with the other. 'You been jacking?'

'What's it to you? You ain't having none.' He opened a tube of hair gel and smoothed it on to his fringe.

She snatched it away from him and shoved him hard. He sprawled gaping at her on the floor, and I registered that he was sitting on the pouting paper face of Justin Timberlake, as featured in glorious *Smash Hits* Technicolor. 'I'll tell you what I'm not having none of, Jesus. I'm not having none of you being brought back by the law again and making this family a laughing stock because you don't know your ragged arse from a store detective. If you give Mum one more grey hair this term, I'm telling Erin Petrovic what a wanker you are. And I don't just mean a thicko, cos she knows that. She don't know the rest –'

JJ was up on his feet in a heartbeat. 'Not Erin, sis! I'm

taking her to the prom next month – and someone saw a tube of spermicide in her satchel –'

Maria smirked, and propelled him through the door. 'In other words, she's a sure thing. Who wouldn't dream of going to the prom, or come to that to the chip shop on the corner, with a pervert who regularly relieves himself over pictures of Carol Vorderman.' She slammed the door and beamed at me. 'I know why they call it *Countdown*. Only takes him five consonants and a vowel from start to finish. Believe me, I've seen the paper towels. Good job they're extra-absorbent.' She sat back down beside me. 'I love this song! It's so crap –' It was 'Crying at the Discotheque' by Alcazar.

'So –' She turned to me, leaning low on her elbows. 'How many times you done it?'

'I don't know –'

'You slag! How many blokes, then?'

'Um – seven,' I said wildly. I realized straightaway it was too many to convince her. I should've said three.

She narrowed her eyes at me. 'I think I know who they are too –'

What the . . . 'Who?'

She sat up and began to count on her fingers. 'There was that miserable one, the stupid one, that shy one, the bloke who always had a cold –' And here she fell on me, tickling me in exactly the right place. 'And then there was Doc, and I forget the other two's names, but I do remember that Snow White gave you a right going over for stealing her boyfriends, you lying cow!'

It was a fair cop; I lay back and took my punishment, fighting for breath between shrieks of laughter. When she finally let me up I was beyond shame.

'I've never done it,' I confessed.

'Get off . . .' She shook her head. 'But you're so pretty . . .'

I felt weird suddenly; hot and cold. I could hear my breath, feel my blood. Like I was playing hide-and-seek, and the person looking for me had just come into the room.

'Still, that's not saying nothing. The worst slags are usually the mingers. So boys'll like 'em. Never works,' she said sagely. Then she stared at me, the first full-on frank look I think she'd ever given me. She was big on squinting and sneering, narrowing and rolling her eyes. 'Know what? I'll so kill you if you spread it, but I don't know if I've done it or not!'

It was so weird and outrageous, it had to be true. 'But . . . how?'

She shrugged, but looked anything but despondent; looking back, Maria Sweet was actually the only person I've ever known who had so much vitality, so much sparkle, that even that definitely droopy gesture, the shrug, looked dynamic and full of mischievous energy when she did it. Her eyes glinted with a combination of memory and desire. 'Drink, innit? Do God knows what at parties and can't remember a thing the next day.'

'But don't people tell you – at school, I mean –'

She snorted and tossed her hair. 'School! Do me a favour! Think I party with a bunch of kids? Na, I party up

44

in Whitehawk – round the clubs – sometimes with the language students – the Frogs,' she elaborated helpfully. ''Sides,' she added cheerfully, 'they're all as pissed as I am. They don't know nothing! Speaking of which –' She pulled open her dressing-table drawer and pulled out a half-bottle of Smirnoff. 'Fancy a nip?'

'On a school night?' I couldn't help it.

'On a school night!' Sugar lisped with horrid accuracy. Well, it was exaggerated, but the spirit was spot-on. 'Yeth, on a school night, Kimmy-Lou! And I might even pop a couple of Pro Plus too!' She added a good belt of vodka to her Tango, and then tilted the bottle over my glass, turning to look me straight in the eye. It was crunch time.

I think I could have been sensible if at that moment the silence hadn't been broken as the next song came on, and it was one I've always loved even though in theory I didn't have time for dance music. It was that old tune by Ultra Nate, 'Free', and the opening chords of it, so yearning and sweet and wild, made me grab the bottle from her hand and add a massive shot to my virgin soda. I picked it up and drank it down, then stared her straight in the eye.

'Where's the Pro Plus then? Or are you all talk, Sweet?'

She whooped, drained her glass, pulled me to my feet. She turned me to face the mirror, stood behind me, caught my wrists in her hands and began to move my arms wildly to that beautiful song – 'Cos you're FREE – to do what you WANT to do – you gotta LIVE YOUR LIFE – do what you WANT to do!' Her eyes were wide in mock horror.

'Ohmigod, Kim! Look! You're just a dancing machine!

A slave to the rhythm! You just can't control your feet! You're going to dance yourself to death! Stop! STOP! NOT ON A SCHOOL NIGHT, KIM!'

We fell backwards on to her bed, helpless with laughter – and in my case, rising nausea from unfamiliar Smirnoff on an empty stomach, bar a Belgian waffle – and it could have gone either way right then; I could have vomited or I could have fallen in love. As it turned out, I went for the latter option. But I often wish I'd just been sick, right there and then on Sugar's sweet-smelling GirlWorld bed, and disgraced myself with short, sharp shame, rather than take the scenic route to sorrow, as I was later to do. But again, I get ahead of myself. There were loads of good times to come, before the morning after – that final morning after, the one that never ends – finally caught up with us.

5

'I feel like crap. Thank God it's Friday,' moaned a bleary-eyed Sugar the next morning as we straggled into assembly. 'It's so unfair. Why do I always have to be the one who suffers for the stuff I do?'

'Cause and effect?' I suggested, and she pinched me hard on the waist. Sparkles of joy shot through me. I wondered if I dared risk it and try to goad her into a proper duffing-up at break, or if I'd get more satisfaction from just looking at her. I decided to try the latter and pulled a roll of Nurofen out of my pocket.

Sugar grabbed them and swallowed down two, then a third. I was horrified.

'You shouldn't take three! It's exceeding the stated dose!'

'Ith extheeding the stateth dothe!' she mocked. I honestly don't have a lisp. 'I'll take another three in half an hour if my head don't feel better. These things are like sweets to me. Ever had ProPain?'

I shook my head. They didn't sound nice. Like they would make your pain worse.

'They're cool – got codeine in. Two of them with a vodka and Bull, you're flying. You got to get them from the pharmacy though, tight bastards. My mum's got some in her handbag – well, she did have, till I nicked 'em!'

'You took them last night? But you knew it was a school night –'

She rolled her eyes. 'Give me strength! You're a right little party animal, aintcha, Kizzy? Talking of which –' She leaned close – 'Big one tonight. French student I met at the Paradox last week. You up for it?'

'What time will it end?'

She laughed wickedly. 'When I've had e-bloody-nough, baby girl, that's when!'

'My dad –'

'Tell him you're sleeping at mine.'

'I don't know –'

'OK.' She looked around and caught the eye of a tall, skinny, blonde girl, Jolie French, the only girl in our year to come remotely close to her in terms of looks. Jolie had come down from London less than a year before and already had her own little fan club, having acquired a lot of Maria's drones when they bailed out; despite this, you could tell she wanted to be friends with Sugar and would chuck them all in a heartbeat for the chance to hang out with her. Up till now though, Sugar had acted as if she didn't exist.

'Hey, Jolie, you want to –'

'What time shall I call for you?' I hissed, grabbing her by the arm and marching her on.

She looked smug, but not at all surprised. 'Swing by at eight. We'll have a bit of a sesh while we're getting ready.'

'What shall I wear?'

She sniggered. 'If you can wear it, it ain't the right thing. You got anything your dad hates seeing you in?'

I thought about it. 'He doesn't like crop tops –'

'Chuck everything he doesn't like into a bag and bring it. We'll sort you out.'

We filed into the assembly hall and faced the front. Sugar's face was turned towards the stage as she spoke. 'Only don't bring nothing you really want to keep. Cos the chances are it'll be a write-off after tonight.'

I suppose you're wondering why I'm not more het up about my new feelings for Maria. Well, I told you I was level-headed, didn't I, and naturally as a good little library-ticket-holding girl with liberal parents I've read all those novels which bend over backwards to reassure you that it's perfectly normal for your haywire hormones to make you believe that you're in love with your same-sex role model. Whatever.

It was 'only natural', wasn't it, to get a crush on someone of the same sex who seemed to have all the qualities – beauty, confidence, absence of parent who brought oversized jars with French words written on them into the house, thus driving away other parent – that you wanted for yourself? If you really WERE a proper gay teenager, you'd get so much I-hear-you-and-it's-only-natural-at-your-age eyewash from parents and agony aunts about loving someone of the same gender that you could easily end up totally confused and isolated, in fact more so than years ago, when they were telling you it was a filthy sin.

Poor gay teenagers! I thought smugly as I eyed my treacherous, respectable self in my bedroom mirror. So lonely, so sad, so . . . stuck. Not like me, who's totally on top of her totally temporary pash for the naughtiest girl in the school. I checked my bookbag: crop top, low-rise Levi's, high-rise hair gel, heels. I thought of Maria, getting ready in her bedroom in Ravendene, and how she would look tonight.

Then my stomach flipped over, like on the scariest ride in the theme park, and I ran to the bathroom to be sick.

6

I could feel the music throbbing in my veins. Sugar caught my eye and crossed the room to where I sprawled on the stuffing-shedding sofa. She was more beautiful than I had ever seen her. Her semi-exposed breasts as she bent over me were a hand's span from my face, and she looked at me with the biggest, softest eyes in the world. I gazed back, all my soul reaching out through its windows to stroke hers. Then she spoke.

'I lost my effing skirt! Some bitch got me to swap in the toilet and now I'm landed with these minging culottes!'

She slumped down next to me and swigged her Bacardi Breezer resignedly. I giggled and sipped my Red Square (sensible Kimmy; even when getting drunk at a party her dad doesn't know she's at she's sure to take a drink that's got stimulants to balance the intoxicants!).

'Why d'you do it then?' They really were minging – blue-and-white striped – even on her.

'Give me a bite of an E, din' she? Can't even feel nothing now.' She looked very sad for a moment. Then mischief hit her face like dark sunlight. 'But I'm buggered if I'm gonna wear 'em. I fancy that Frenchie, that Daveed, something rotten. I'm never gonna pull him looking like a lesbo.' She stood up and began to fumble at her ignoble waistband.

'Sugar!' I protested. But not too much. I thought

about the absent skirt. It wasn't as if anyone would notice the difference if she was stripped from the waist down . . .

When I'd turned up at the Sweet house three hours earlier, I wondered if I'd ever seen anyone in the flesh who was wearing less than Sugar, bar myself after a bath. The black boob tube was more of a cummerbund and the gold-sequinned skirt seemed to have made its excuses and left some time ago. Add perfect breasts and endless legs and top with a face from your dreams and hair from your worst, most envious nightmare and we're talking walking sex. I just stood there in my sensible sportswear and gaped.

But you'd think she was dressed up in a white communion frock topped with a priceless tiara and a bridal veil the way the Sweet females were reacting.

She-Ra and Evil-Lyn danced around her, touching her hem – if indeed the so-called skirt was big enough to have one – and coming out with blatant untruths such as 'Ooh, 'Ria, you look like a princess!' while Suzy, who had just answered the door and led me into the 'lounge', smiled serenely at the profoundly sexually depraved tableau in front of her.

'You look just like Britney, love!'

Maria sneered and tossed her glossy hair. 'Don' wan' look like that old bag!' But you could tell she was pleased. Till she took in what I was wearing.

'Jeez, Kiz, who died?'

Suzy and the twins turned and looked at me in mute disapproval. I was wearing a hoodie and tracksuit bottoms, perfectly reasonable camouflage, but about as welcome and enviable as a traffic-warden's uniform in the Sweet household. I held up my bookbag. 'I brought my stuff –'

'Great. Let's go up to mine.' She graciously allowed the twins to stroke her sequins one last time before grabbing my hand and hauling me through the door.

Up in her room she took my bag and emptied it on to the bed. She poked at the jeans and the red crop top, her face like a dismayed child on Christmas Day, who's just unwrapped a Ker-Plunk they thought was going to be a GameCube.

'Ooh . . . yeah, thass good, I s'pose, keepin' it . . . real.' She turned to me, as businesslike as a girl can be who's dressed for lap-dancing. 'Get your kit off then. Let's get the party started.'

I turned my back and changed my clothes, but she wasn't even looking. She was fiddling with her CD player – Sounds of Eden came on. I turned around and she straightened up and burst out laughing.

'Kimber-LEY!'

'What?' She thinks I'm ugly, she thinks I'm minging, how could she think anything else looking like that?

'Your TITS! Bloody amazing! Tell you what, I could fancy you myself.'

I felt like crying and kissing her, both. 'They look grotesque, don't they?'

'They look wicked – totally porno though.'

I could feel myself getting as red as my top. 'I hate that – but there's nothing I can do with them.'

'Chill – chill!' She narrowed her eyes at me. Then, 'Swap tops!'

'What –' But she was already pulling her boob tube over her head. I won't tell you exactly how I felt at that moment, because it now seems as unreal as being tiny and believing in fairies. But it was like all the rushing in the world, the rushing of the ocean and the breeze and the blood in my ears, and what I imagined the rush of drugs to be like too – scary but brilliant – all happening at once. And all that rushing should have knocked me over, but the very force, coming from all directions, held me up. It's like I was under water, yet also on top of the world looking down, as she reached out, the bit of black material in her hand, turned me round, pulled my top over my head –

'Put your arms up. That's right –' And unhooked my bra. I leaned forward, dazed, to shake it off and she slid her tube down my body. Then she turned me round.

She was still topless. And now, as if that wasn't agony enough, she was smiling like a proud parent. Or like a pet owner whose mutt has just won Best of Breed at Crufts.

'Excellent!' She twirled me to face the mirror. 'See? Still hot, but the Lycra holds 'em in. Look –'

I looked. And I saw that I looked good. I saw a short-ish blonde girl with a round, big-eyed face and a slim but curvy body packed compactly into jeans and black Lycra. But more than anything I saw the narrow brown back of the most beautiful girl in the world disappearing into a red crop top. And all I wanted was to know when she would next take it off, and all I knew was that I would have cut off my little finger – left hand, let's not go mad here – right then and there for a guarantee of being there when she did so.

But now she was taking off those tragic culottes, grasping at my knee as she did so, trying to stand on one leg. 'Sod it – shtop moving, Kim –'

'I'm perfectly shtill – still,' I hiccuped. 'It's shoe whosh moving –'

'Frig it!' She tripped over her culotte-bound ankles and toppled on to me. 'Ah, forge' it . . . just gon' have a sleep . . .'

She closed her eyes, lying across my lap, and something unusual happened to me. I sobered up in a second, and I decided, for once in my life, to do something that might well – shock horror! – draw attention to me. I didn't even have to try, to struggle to get my courage up; maybe it was the Red Square or maybe it was love, crush, friendship, whatever you want to call it, but I wasn't going to have Maria laughed at by these snotty foreign students, passed out half-dressed and sprawled over me. Even though having her half-dressed sprawled over me made my toes curl inside my strappy Faith sandals.

I was going to be the Kim I always was – selfless, sensible, considerate. Even better, I was going to get my hands all over her. I was going to pull her culottes back up.

'Sugar.' I spoke low and urgently. She opened her eyes and gave me a dopey, adorable smile, then closed them again. 'Sugar!' I shook her. 'Sit up straight!'

Her eyes opened wide for a second. 'It wasn't me!' she said indignantly. Then they closed. She began to snore prettily.

I could feel the French students' amusement from across the room as they danced casually to Air. I could see that noncy, superior Davide, apparently the current object of Sugar's affections, leading the smirking smorgasbord. He whispered something to a slender, sweatered, straight-haired girl, about eighteen like him, wearing no make-up and looking like an AWOL supermodel; I just knew she was French. She looked at Sugar and smiled, whispering back to him.

Something snapped. And I slapped Sugar's face, hard. Her eyes flew open. 'What the –'

'UP!' I hissed. 'You sit the frig up RIGHT NOW! Or I'll hit you so hard you won't –'

In answer, she pulled my head down and kissed me hard on the lips. Fireworks exploded inside me.

To this day I don't know why she did it. Was she just so drunk she had no idea of what she was doing? Was she not drunk at all, and was this a sure way of attracting Davide's attention where taking off her trousers had failed? Did she – oh, please! – did she just want to kiss me?

Well, I never got a chance to ask, because there was Jean-Jacques Smoothie right in front of us. Never seen anyone move so fast. And Sleeping Beauty smiling goofily into his eyes.

'You 'ave slip, yes?' He HAD to be putting that accent on.

'Beddy-byes,' Sugar agreed. I thought I was going to hurl, right then and there, over the pair of them.

'You wan' proper slip upstairs?' He couldn't be for real!

Well, all I can say is that Sugar suddenly seemed totally sober, standing up smartly and peeling off those bloody culottes that had caused all the trouble in the first place, like a seasoned chef on speed stripping a tiger prawn. Before you could say 'two-faced bitch from hell' she was out of that room and up the stairs with the garlic-gargler as though she'd been in training for the event for a good six months. I sat there poleaxed on the sofa. Even the spilling stuffing seemed to mock me now, or maybe echo me – superfluous to requirements, best ignored, an embarrassment.

Then I caught the French girl's eye, and her disappointment – worn as only a girl who has never been disappointed would wear it – cheered me up no end. So it wasn't only me! I laughed, raised my Red Square, swigged soundly and passed out.

'Was he any cop then?'

Sugar groaned and ground her face against the wall. 'Kiz . . . what a question to ask!'

Everyone in the playground was looking; not looking up at Sugar Sweet, the way they used to, but looking on, amused. I put my hand on her shoulder and turned her face away from their view; she turned easily.

'Rubbish, was he?'

'C'mon, Kiz! What do I do, eh? I DON'T REMEM-BER! You do the maths. NO CHANGE!'

'Oh. I see.' I had to cover my mouth and cough to hide my smile.

'Well, I bloody wish I did –'

'Chill, chill.' I patted her shoulder patronizingly. 'You'll be fine –'

'But I tell you what I do remember, Kim.' She whirled on me, pushing against the wall with the heel of her hand, and damn me if even with bloodshot eyes and blotchy skin she wasn't the most natural-born, bona-fide beauty I could ever have imagined. 'I remember that you were a really good snog, that's what I remember. You want to watch yourself, you do.' She caught my chin in her hand, narrowed her eyes and made a kissy mouth at me. 'Or you gonna get yourself a rep, that's what you'll get. And on a school night too –'

I don't know what would have happened if at that moment a ferret-faced first year hadn't come running up to us, and panted, 'Kim Lewis! I been looking for you everywhere. The Rock wants you. Now!'

I've been so obsessed with Sugar, I haven't told you about The Rock. This is Mrs Rockminster, the new head teacher who turned up at Ravendene about the same time I did, who's meant to turn the school around. I mean, YEAH RIGHT! Mrs Rockminster is a bit of a mystery to all us kids – that is, if any of us ever admitted there's such a thing as a mystery, like there's one thing we don't understand.

Unlike the previous head, some sad dad who tried to get real with da kidz and paid the price, she's made us respect her by keeping her distance while she sorts out what she thinks of us.

So when I knock on her door, I'm a bit clueless. And quite surprised when instead of calling, 'Come in,' she opens the door herself and smiles at me.

'Kim. Thank you. Please come in. Sit down.'

Her room's not the usual top teacher's retreat either – not scared and spartan and always under pressure – but more like a doctor's, an olde-worlde bloke with a name like Fahey or Donahue perhaps, quite fond of the grog and with framed photos of his daughters (Caitlin, Bernadette) on his desk. It's a room in which everyone instinctively knows their place; I take the hard chair opposite the bigger, padded one.

She takes her place and rests her forearms lightly on the table, her hands making not quite a steeple, more a sort of little annexy bit. 'To begin with, Kim, is there anything YOU'D like to discuss?'

Um, I think I'm in love with a crazy girl who may or may not have slept with half the boys in East Brighton but who is definitely well on the way to alcoholic poisoning, and I don't know whether to encourage her drinking so I can possibly get off with her when she's off her face one night, or try to stop her because I'm, like, her friend?

'Um, I don't think so . . .'

'Well, let's see. It must have been quite a shock for you at first, coming here from Preston High –'

59

'Oh, you know. Not really.' She looked encouraging. It seemed mean not to give her what she wanted. 'Teenagers, you know . . . pretty much the same everywhere really.'

'Nevertheless, to come from a private girls' school to a mixed comprehensive –'

I forgot she was prompting me and waited for her to finish, feeling quite interested in what she was going to say. I honestly couldn't see myself that there was a massive difference between the school I'd left and the school I now attended; at Ravendene the kids didn't take their schooling so seriously, swore more and were more likely to thump you if they thought you were a wuss, but in many ways it was far less stressful than the High, less harsh. The pressure to succeed academically at my old school had been mad, and the lust to come first at all times pretty much stamped out any sense of camaraderie. For instance, kids at Ravendene shared and copied homework all the time, but you never saw that at Preston, even between alleged best friends.

Another thing I'd noticed: I know that teenage girls are meant to be more relaxed and less looks-conscious in single-sex schools, but the girls at Preston were so aware of their superior status and so used to having the idea of excellence in every aspect of their lives drummed into them that they took one-upmanship out of the classroom and into the corridors and cloakrooms, which often served as catwalks on which the thin, pretty, sophisticated girls showed off mercilessly in front of the plain ones. The girls at Ravendene may have slapped the make-up on thicker, but they seemed far more cheerful about their looks, plain and pretty alike – there wasn't that joyless desire for perfection that made the air at my old school crackle with tension. And though they may have drunk more, and come to school with hangovers more often, there certainly wasn't the amount of chucking up in the toilets that went on at the High, particularly after lunch. It's a known fact that anorexia and bulimia strike the type of girls who strive for excellence – pernickety perfectionists to whom getting the perfect grade A and fitting into a size-six dress are two faces of the same coin. For the same reason, even the smoking of the Preston girls was grim and medicinal, something done to suppress appetites rather than put up two fingers at the grown-ups.

So, no, I didn't have that many complaints. And if I had, I certainly wasn't about to tell a sadult! I smiled brightly and shrugged.

'I'm fine.'

Fine! If only adults could get behind this word – see it as the bright-white dust cover it is, hiding from them all the things we know they're too wussy to deal with. We wear this all-purpose disguise like little ghosts because they've already screwed up their own lives so chronically that we know they only need one more strand of information and bang, goodbye! So we wear all this cover-up and say we're 'fine', even right up to the trapdoor, when we kick the chair away and hopefully go to a better place where nothing can touch us any more. And then we leave a note asking THEM, the sadults, to forgive US! I mean, as if!

'Couldn't be better,' I added for extra emphasis.

'Good.' She gave me a look. For a minute I thought she could see right through me. 'Excellent. Well, in that case, I'm sure the exchange won't hold any problems for you –'

'Exchange?' I sat bolt upright. For some weird reason I had this sudden image of myself being swapped for a foreign student without benefit of prior knowledge, and she'd sleep in my bed and use my pore-strips and everything while I had to make do with a pile of straw or some-thing in a rough Normandy outhouse. After a nanosecond of course I realized that was nuts, but it shows you the low opinion I've got of grown-ups and the way they move the goalposts without telling you, for their own convenience. Well, I'd had a two-parent family swapped for the one-parent model without consultation; if they could take my mum away, what else might they do?

'The public-and-private-school exchange scheme. You haven't heard of it, Kim?'

Go on, rub it in. That I'm an ignorant Raver who's only clued up on what seafront bars are running the Red Light Rush (half-price drinks, if you're interested, when the red light flashes) at any given time, and no longer a Preston High-brow who's totally genned up on the latest initiatives in the public-private social alliance. 'Uhhh . . .'

The Rock sighed and smiled gamely. 'Rich and poor, Kim . . . it's a problem in every city. Especially amongst young people, just starting out in life, being told that studying, buckling down, working hard is the way to find fulfilment and material success. And then the young people at the lower end of the social scale, especially the bright ones, realize that they've only been given a little bit of the information. That someone's been a bit economical with the truth. And that it's not just how hard they work at school but also the postcode of that school which is going to make a big difference to their lives. To whether they get the life they want, and deserve. Are you following me?'

I nodded, a bit numb. I was getting the Life Isn't Fair talk! Grown-ups, couldn't you just wrap 'em up and eat 'em?

'So – hence 'S'Cool-Swap.' The Rock looked at me proudly and I knew I was missing something in translation. So I looked curious and, damn, I wished to heck I hadn't when she literally spelt it out. 'S – apostrophe – COOL. S'COOL! As in, "It's cool!" To swap schools!'

I'm not an emotional person, but I swear I wanted to break down and cry when she said this so proudly. For me, for her, for the whole darn world, but especially for the English language. But I pulled myself together and managed to say, 'OK . . .' I still didn't get what she wanted from me.

She cleared her throat. In my experience people only clear their throats when they're trying to make room for a whole lot of new rubbish. 'Kim – the school that we've been chosen to work with is Preston High.' She looked at me as though I was an optician's chart she was trying to decipher, and she'd got stuck on the third line. 'We'll be joining the class you used to be in, and they'll be joining us. Are you going to be all right with that?'

They do this, see. Sadults. They ask your opinion on what they're going to do anyway, and it's just about as important, your view, as whether or not you want an avalanche to fall on you. But at least an avalanche doesn't muck around with your feelings, pretending they're important. I just felt blank, sunk; baffled and sure both at once.

So I just nodded my head, my clean, blonde, clever, Kim-type head. 'Bring it on,' I said.

7

Maria Sweet pushed me against the wall and got down on to her knees in front of me. It was a hot day, her knees were bare beneath her blue-checked school dress and I knew the right one had a scar on it where she'd fallen off her bike at the age of eight. It was the most beautiful scar in the world, I'd bet my CD collection on it – even the signed Dido. She looked up at me; 'Pull it up!' she ordered in her heartbreaking rasp.

I pulled the hem halfway up my thighs and stopped. She drew in her breath in irritation, grabbed the thin material in her hand and pulled it up all the way; I was really embarrassed because it was a Monday and my knickers said Friday – ever the nit-picker, me. I swallowed hard as her head moved in towards my thighs.

Then I felt the jab of the tweezers and it was all over.

'Got it!' She dropped my dress and held up the tweezers to the sun. 'Little buggers, bees. What's their problem?' She laughed throatily. 'Still, it'd be good though, wouldn't it? Putting your sting in someone . . .'

You have, Maria, you have!

'Come on.' She got to her feet and took my hand. 'Let's go and have that blunt. Gonna need it, hanging with Princess Thing and Little Miss . . . That,' she trailed off weakly.

'They're just ordinary girls,' I laughed as we went

65

deeper into Preston Park. She looked at me contemptuously. 'Kim. They PAY to go to school! That's bloody weird.'

We sat down by a big tree, but not the one I'd been sprawling in the shade of when that bee took a shine to me. It was noon on a school day, we'd been given the morning off and we were due at Preston High in an hour, where half our year – the female half – would be honoured with a peek at private education while half their year roughed it over at Ravendene Comp, no doubt learning how to forge prescriptions and get pregnant.

Maria thought the whole thing a hoot, and one which would no doubt be amplified by a quick smoke in the park. As I watched her finesse the joint, tweaking and smoothing it, proud of her handiwork, I wished the teacher who had recently proclaimed her one hundred per cent free of arts and crafts skills in front of the whole class could see her now. Or maybe not.

She lit up and inhaled. 'So . . . who's the daddy, then? At this school of yours.'

I laughed. 'The what?'

'Queen Bee, Queen Bitch, whatever. Who's the bitch I got to stare out to make the ghost-girls go "Oo!"'

'I don't know,' I said. Of course, I was praying Zoe wouldn't be there; of course, Maria read my mind.

'It's your girl, innit? That black girl. One you always go on about when you're pissed-up –'

'I SO do not!' I grabbed the joint from her, sucked it savagely, came up coughing like a first year.

She laughed, taking it from me and wiping it on her

hem. 'Not like that, Kimmy-Lou. Did they teach you that at pay-school? Like this – slowly.' She did some snaky thing, hissing, but backwards.

I did it too and I was suddenly flooded with warmth, both physically and mentally. I lay back and the park, no, the WORLD, seemed to shift and shrug suggestively around me. The branches above me fell away kindly so that the sun could shine even more sweetly upon my lovely face, and I had the strangest and yet most weirdly sexy feeling that all around me the park, all the bits I couldn't see, were changing places – not in a nasty way to confuse and alarm me, but mischievously to delight and amuse me. I sighed and wriggled with sleepy pleasure.

So yeah, I suppose you could say I liked drugs . . .

'Yeah,' she continued dreamily, 'it's that Zoe one. Upset my Kimmy, she did. And anyone who upsets my Kimmy upsets . . . me . . .'

I sat up and looked at her. Her eyes were even longer and deeper than ever, and her voice was soft, but she wasn't laid-back, chilled-out, loved-up or any of the other things smoking dope's meant to make you. Maria was the opposite of a shape-shifter, I'd worked that much out; speed and booze and blunts merely made her more herself, but more dangerous, as the real razor-sharp Sugar hid behind her temporary friend, Sweetie, who simply APPEARED to be under the influence of something softening. Then at the eleventh hour, when you'd finally let down your guard, Sugar would jump out from Sweetie's shadow and throw back at you all the foolish things you'd said when you were

67

out of it. The only way she did change when intoxicated was sexually, when every trace of the sharp Sugar was dissolved in desire and amnesia. But I didn't want to think about that right now.

'I don't talk about Zoe –' I insisted.

'Yeah.' She snatched the blunt back. 'You do. You so do, Kim, when you're on one. On and on and on. And I don't know if I don't like this Zoe because you hate her – or because you love her.' She squinted at me through the smoke and smiled. 'It's horrible, innit? This situation. It's so, SO gay.'

Gay. I hate the way we use that word these days. Just means anything we don't like, anything that's not cool, and as we're fifteen that's about ninety per cent of everything. So socks are gay, spots are gay, science is gay – I mean, I'm not arguing here, they ARE all gay. But things being the way they are, with my heart and stuff, I don't need my possible future sexual identity bandied about as a byword for everything that's rubbish. Then, when Maria uses it like that, which 'gay' does she mean? Does she mean she's got gay feelings about me? Or does she just mean it's rubbish to have old and new best friends meeting up? Well, I'll vouch for that one. But as if the whole gay thing wasn't confusing enough already – did it really need this? Gay is the new sad – it's official!

I lunged for the blunt, not wanting to think any more, but Sugar held it away and sprung up on to her knees. 'Close your eyes a minute.'

'Get lost – give me that –'

68

'Just do it!'

'OK.' I knelt up level with her and closed my eyes. I expected the wrong end of the joint in my mouth, and some sort of exotic blow-back like I'd heard about.

Instead I tasted chips and vanilla and the darting teasing taste of a tongue between my lips, only slightly marred by tobacco and skunk. And then I heard the whisper in my ear; 'Oops, I've got a cold sore. Hope it's not herpes!' And then the laughter of the two most brilliant, beautiful girls in Brighton as I jumped to my feet and chased her through a park that might have looked as though it suffered from dog-mess and syringes and the usual scabby flotsam of modern life but was in fact the Garden of Eden Mark Two, only better this time, with no stupid man in it to stop us having fun, to make us boring, to make us old before our time.

'You look older,' said Saint, and if ever you can imagine one girl saying that to another one in a way that isn't favourable, this was it. I didn't look older as in boyfriends, clubbing, uni; I looked older as in boring, tired, over.

We were standing outside the assembly hall waiting to go in, and fate had shoved me right up against my ex-best friend so hard I could smell the Juicy Fruit on her breath. On my other side stood Maria, swaying slightly under the influence of her lunchtime smoke. She was as tall as Saint, and they now looked at each other, very cool, over my head, making me feel that it was only them in this scenario, and me just the stepping stone.

'She's been living it up, is why,' said Maria softly. 'Been

LIVING, really. For the first time.' She smirked. 'I've even got her partying on a school night! Kimmy!'

Zoe smiled at her, and I knew something nasty was coming. 'Well, it's all good, I guess. But it won't do much for her future.'

Maria stared at her, amused. And without missing a beat – 'Yeah, but on the other hand, maybe she don't need a future. Cos now she's got a LIFE. Right here, right now.'

Her, she – who was I, the cat's mute mother? 'I can *speak* –' I started up indignantly, but I had thin air against me. It was hard to hear up there on Teen Olympus. And the crowd had started moving forward into the hall.

'She's not gonna have much of a life when she leaves school with no results and has to get a job in Asda.'

'What, not like every stuck-up ex-student in this town with a degree they might as well dip in detergent and use as a Wet Wipe, who's stuck on the end of the pier making the Crusherator go round!'

Sugar had a point; Saint scowled. Sugar turned her eyes demurely towards the stage as Mrs Clune walked on. 'Let's talk about it later, give you time to think of an answer. Your top bird's about to go off.'

Saint shot me this look like, 'It's all your fault.' Typical! She wasn't going the right way to win me over, I thought. And then it occurred to me that that was probably neither here nor there to her! At least Sugar cared what I thought, even if she was usually too drunk or stoned to remember the next day.

'Good afternoon, everybody.' Mrs Clune favoured the

room with one of her stern yet sexy smiles. With her red hair and smart jacket she looked like a newsreader. 'On behalf of the girls of Preston High, I'd like to welcome the girls of Ravendene Comprehensive in what I hope and believe will be the first of many such exchanges.'

Maria sniggered and Saint scowled.

'Our city has seen many changes over the past few years – for example, the huge influx of Londoners. And then there is the ongoing process of inclusion – and I use the word inclusion, not tolerance, which implies that the majority is doing the minority a favour rather than being empowered by them – towards all the groups which make our city by the sea so special. People of all enriching cultures and sexualities.'

'Gaylords,' whispered Maria, just loud enough for Saint to hear. 'Them and gyppos. Ain't her who has to clean up the mess after them, is it! And I bet her dog never choked on a condom down Duke's Mound –'

'Change is not just inevitable – change is good,' Mrs Clune continued, blithely unaware of this slur on her street cred. 'But change can only be truly successful if what already stands is fully respected and utilized in the realization of all that we can be – together and as individuals. In the race to promote the place we live in as a feel-good paradise, the great gulf between our affluent and disadvantaged citizens must not be glossed over with catchy slogans and breezy jingles. And we must remember that the future of our city is our youth, far more than brave new industries and challenging social programmes. With all that in mind, let this be the first of many demonstrations of respect and unity between our two schools.' She stepped back looking pleased with herself.

'What a performer,' whispered Maria as we turned around to file out. 'She's waiting for her round of applause and a nice bunch of daffs, innit!'

'What are we doing first?' I asked Saint politely.

'Art.' She was looking for someone. I couldn't believe it when she raised her hand. 'Paz! Over here!'

Honestly, if Saint had chosen a self-mutilating chickpea on a fork to replace me as her bezzie, I would have been less shocked. Polly Hobart was the girl you could never remember the name of when you look at school photos years later; the girl who couldn't be called unpopular because no one ever gets to know her well enough to find out whether she's likeable or not. Waits for years to take home the class gerbil for the holidays and when she does it dies. Probably her cat eats it.

But here she was, ambling over to us like the cat who got the gerbil AND the cream. It was like her whole body was smirking. At last she had a distinguishing mark! – cos up till then, the one way you could have described her was 'middling'. Middling height, middling weight, middling colouring; I honestly wouldn't have been shocked if I'd found out that her middle name was Middling. She smirked to a standstill in front of me and stared up at Saint like a smirking dog looking at a bone a good six inches bigger than itself.

'This is Polly Hobart,' I told Maria. 'Maria Sweet,' I

told Polly. 'Paz', as it was apparently now called, nodded, sucking her teeth. 'Wassup, Kimbo?' she smirked.

'Well, it's certainly not your fashion sense, Miss Thing,' Sugar shot back. 'What you wearing on your head?'

I looked closer at Polly. I'd thought it was a weird sort of wiry wool hat. But it was her hair; her formerly middling brown, middling wavy hair was teased into the most amazing bird's nest. It was as if she had a huge pubes on her head.

She stroked it protectively. 'I really wanted dreads – dumb-ass school says I can't. But I be bustin' loose any day now –'

'Get moving, will you, Kim? I don't need Parsons on my case,' muttered Saint, hustling me in the direction of the art rooms. But Sugar and I had heard enough to be staring at Polly Hobart in pure molten glee. It WAS – it really WAS! – a genuine 'wigga', right in front of us! I mean, you've always heard about them – white teenagers who go around trying to act like homies – but like the Easter bunny and the Tooth Fairy, they just seem too wonderful to be true. Ooh, the sport we could have with her!

'So, Polly . . . or can I call you Po-Ho, like your homies do?' said Maria with lethal slowness as we filed into the classroom. Saint looked around urgently for two isolated seats, but we were the first there and had to take an empty table for four, as they all were. 'Where you be hangin'? Where you be partay-ing of an evening?'

Polly looked ill at ease – half glad to be addressed in her adopted tongue, half aware that Saint was on edge. 'All over . . . whatever . . . it's all gravy . . .' she started.

73

'Cos, check this, I know a joint that's always full of playas, and I think it would really, know wha'mean, ring your bell . . .'

'Where it be?' asked Polly innocently.

Maria leaned across the table, her strong, savage teeth revealed in a snarl of glee. 'It be the local A & E, that's where it be! And they've got the technology to remove that dirty great muff off your head!'

It got worse from then on. Our hopefully happy hour of peacefully executing a perfect pencil drawing of a chessboard with scattered pieces was interrupted with grumbles from Maria as she peered across the table, pursing her lips and shaking her head and demanding to know why 'Po-Ho', as she insisted on calling her, had seen fit to leave half the squares white – 'Wassup, you ashamed of your race, baby girl?' I vainly attempted to hold her back as she leaned over and tried to colour in a white square with her black pencil. 'Got to SHOW-WHITEY-WHO-DA-MAN!'

'Maria, STOP it!' I begged. She fell back in her chair, shaking with that silent laughter that summed her up so well; so high on her own badness, so complete and self-contained, so far beyond such minor considerations as rules, regulations and her best friend's excruciating embarrassment. Across the table Polly rubbed out the scribble and Zoe glared at us. Maria looked up, caught her eye and made a kissy face. Saint's glorious toffee skin went a good shade paler and I could tell it was taking a good deal of backbone not to leap across the table and smack Sugar a good one.

We weren't saved by the bell but by Miss Parsons, bless

her, anticipating it by a good five minutes and clapping her hands. 'Class, and Ravendene guests, before you leave today I'm going to set you some . . . homework isn't the word, really, because I'm sure it'll prove to be more fun than effort.' Maria blew a raspberry, then looked around indignantly as if seeking out the culprit. Miss Parsons wisely ignored her.

'What I'd like you each to do, over the next three weeks, is to imagine an alternative reality, inhabited by characters from your imagination. They can be people, animals, machines even – just draw me four examples and write a brief description of each. It can be a utopia or a dystopia – that's less important to me than originality and empathy. No matter how outlandish your creations, I want to feel that, however briefly, you've been under their skin and found out what makes them tick.' She looked at her watch. 'That's it, then –' and the bell rang.

I stood up and tried to hustle Sugar away from Saint and her shameful sidekick, but she wasn't having any – her fun had just begun. She had that devil-light in her eye, and that snaky smoothness in her moves – she looked like a Slinky all ready to go off, that or a beautiful, dangerous, deceptively quiet firework just waiting for someone to come too close. Besides, we had to follow them – we didn't know what came next.

The class was moving back towards the assembly hall.

'What's happening?' I asked Saint.

She looked at me contemptuously. 'Something that'll give your racist friend a real field day, no problem.'

'I heard that,' said Maria loudly.

'You were meant to.' Saint stopped and Po-Ho cannoned into her; so did Sugar, and I followed Polly's example. We stood there blocking the corridor with our bad vibes as the rest of the class seeped timidly around us.

'I'm not no racist,' said Maria passionately. I felt proud of her. Then she sniggered. 'I can't even drive.'

Saint sneered at her; then at me. 'Congratulations, Kim – looks like you got yourself hooked up in record time with the most blatant, ignorant bigot in Ravendene. And that's quite an achievement, from what I hear.'

'What you HEAR?' Maria's voice was loud; people were looking. 'What you HEAR about where I come from? I bet you do! Not that you'd have ever heard us for yourself, or seen us – wouldn't be caught dead there, would you, you stuck-up cow? Well, THAT'S ignorance – just believing what you hear about a bunch of people you've never even met for yourself. And why that's worse than being a racist, I'm afraid I just don't get. So yeah, you're right – maybe I AM ignorant. And I hope I stay that way, rather than end up a know-all bitch like you.'

'Don't try to play the underprivileged white-trash card with me,' Saint hissed at her. 'You don't know what it's like to be judged every day of your life because of where you're from –'

'What, Preston Park!' Maria laughed. ''Sides, I didn't say one damn thing to you about your race, whatever it is. It's your homie here I was having a laugh with.' She turned on Polly. 'And it must have been a bloody cold day in Jamaica when she was born.'

Polly held up a hand, palm out. 'Don't even be going there,' she said sternly. 'Because, check dis, we all be coming from Africa back in the day. It be the crib of all mankind. We all be black inside, made of sunshine.' She looked pleased with herself.

Maria looked pleased with her too. 'Is that right then?' she asked Zoe sweetly.

Zoe looked at Polly with total scorn. Then back at Sugar; 'Mankind originated in Africa, yes. I would have thought even you would have been aware of that basic fact.'

'COohl!' Sugar held up her hand to Polly in a high five; the idiot returned it automatically. 'Then I's as black as y'all are!' She poked her face into Saint's. 'And I surely DON'T need lessons in how to refer to my own people. Know wha'mean?'

Zoe glared at us, grabbed Polly and marched ahead; Sugar sniggered, grabbed my hand and romped after them.

It could have been, SHOULD have been a nightmare, what happened next. As we took our seats – last to arrive due to THAT spat, thus forced to sit in the front row – I recognized Ekow, Brighton's foremost professional African dancer, warming up sidestage. Warming up, one hoped, in all senses of the word, seeing as he was stripped to the waist and wearing some sort of ethnic thong. Yet effortlessly he brought it dignity; Stella, seeing him dance once on Open Day, had said that he could have worn a tutu, a snood and clown-feet and still oozed dignity.

Ever since I could remember, the last day of summer term at Preston High had been brightened and lightened even further by the presence of this gorgeous man from the Gold Coast who had been dancing, drumming and story-telling for a living since the age of seven. (What had he left, what had he lost, how could he bear smiling with such end-less sweetness and patience at us rich, dumb English girls?) He'd been picked for Les Ballets Afriques when he was just sixteen; now he was in his twenties and fruitlessly attempting to bring African culture to us well-fed Philistines – part of Mrs Clune's efforts to 'build bridges in the community'.

Now the poor guy wasn't just being wheeled out on the last day of term to titillate a bunch of rich girls, but to pique the interest of the rogue Ravers into the bargain! As he pranced down the steps from the stage, drumming gently all the while, to take up his position in the cleared centre of the assembly hall, I couldn't bring myself to turn my head and look at Sugar; I was just aware of her steely, cold-blooded body leaning forward, everything tensed. And I knew that she was going to say, or do, or even THROW something horrible at Ekow – thereby totally living up, or rather down, to everything that Saint had sneered at us.

I was vaguely aware of Ekow talking about the seasons – some spirits or other – then the running wolf and the pouncing cheetah got a look-in. Whatever, it was a recipe for disaster whichever way you looked at it. Sugar would have a field day with him! The drumming increased in volume and tempo, Maria leaned as far forward in her seat as she could – and then the strangest thing happened. She rose slowly from her seat in the front row and, when I turned to look in horror, I saw that she had the sweetest, softest smile imaginable on her lovely face.

It was all a bit of a blur after that, albeit a gorgeous one; Sugar walking towards Ekow like a sexy sleepwalker, planting each foot slowly and surely, clapping her hands in rhythm with his drumming – Saint and Po-Ho looking dumbstruck, Saint's face quickly becoming a portrait of furious dismay – Sugar drawing level with Ekow, staring at him as his broad smile grew ever bigger – and then the most furious torrent of drumming you've ever heard while Maria danced around him like a thing possessed, her amazing hair billowing and flouncing. Finally, still drumming with one hand, Ekow caught her round the waist with one arm – she did the same with him – and they spun each other round until they were almost indistinguishable. I swear I could hear a hundred girls hold their breath as one.

Then the loudest drumbeat imaginable, like funked-up thunder, and it was all over – Ekow and Maria stood flushed and panting, still entwined. I registered the dumbstruck faces of the teachers, who must have known that 'touching' between girls and performers wasn't allowed in this world or any other, yet who had been powerless to move from the moment the whole strange, beautiful thing started. Then Ekow bowed formally, Maria curtsied and we were pelting out of the hall, out of the school, and into the summer sun of a much smaller and colder world than we'd just been treated to.

I believe the words 'Get her!', 'Up-herself bitch!' and

'Slag!' were tossed from some sorely envious quarters, but we didn't stop to argue, we didn't stop at all until we were back in Preston Park, back under our tree, and we fought over the remains of the joint until it was finished and we lay back, laughing hysterically. I knew Sugar was something, but this? What a way to serve it to them!

She caught hold of me, still giggling, rolled me over and kissed me weakly on the lips. Then she fell away, leaving me blearily blissed out as she stretched her long arms and looked up at the sky. 'Kimbo, I never thought I'd say this. But HECK, it's great being black!'

8

She came out of my bathroom and smiled at me, looking younger than I've ever seen her, wearing a short blue chemise, her hair in a ponytail and a dab of toothpaste on her chin. It was half-past twelve and she was about to climb into my bed, my own innocent Kimmy-type bed, and she wasn't wearing any knickers. I was on a spare futon across the room, but, hey, you can't win 'em all. She took a flying leap – revealing just about everything – into the bed, and burrowed under the covers. She must have seen me staring and got the wrong idea – thank God! – because she fingered her chin gingerly.

'Spot,' she explained helpfully. 'Nothing dries 'em up quicker than toothpaste. And if you got really big bags under your eyes and a hot perving date that night, just put some of that Preparation H under them for half an hour. It's for piles – innit gross?' she elaborated. A look of unutterable dread and sorrow came upon her lovely face. 'But don't get none in your eye – it stings like a bastard.'

I laughed. It was so cute and comic, the way that she always looked at her most ethereal just before she came out with a cussing.

'Where d'you learn all that then, Shug? Finishing school?'

She stuck a swivelling finger up at me, and her tongue out at me. 'Ain't the school on earth that could finish me!'

'Go on!' I goaded her. 'I bet you even know how to get into a car drunk without showing your knickers.'

'Course I do – don't wear none!'

I broke up, and she looked at me approvingly. 'You're all right, you are, Kiz.'

'Gee, um, THANKS.' Heart in throat, foot in mouth. Why couldn't I ever be witty? Or even just thick and cool. 'Milkshakes', Zoe used to call them – the girls who we sometimes stood aside for in the street, who weren't smart yet somehow had IT. Face it, the only IT I was ever going to have was my computer. (As I'm used to my jokes falling flat, I'll just point out that this is a pun on Information Technology. Tragic, isn't it?)

'Your dad's OK too, inee?'

'He liked you as well.' It was true, he had, after the initial double-take at such a level of beauty totally beyond the call of duty when we rolled into the kitchen at sundown after our grand day out and begged him to spring for a couple of stuffed-crusts. I found myself thinking about Zoe again. How it's always the bad girls, paradoxically, the stroppy and self-upping, who charm the parents out of their trees; they've got the front, whereas we nice girls just seem furtive rather than shy, like we've got some shocking codeine habit to hide.

She sat up and hugged her knees. It was an uncharacteristically young gesture, and it made me feel very old. 'Get your dad together with my mum!' she leered. She must have seen the look of involuntary horror on my face, because she swung her legs over the side of the bed and

82

suddenly looked much older. She reached down beside my bed and scrabbled in her backpack, her eyes showing none of their usual mischief and sedition when she held up a half-bottle of Smirnoff. She took a slug and wiped her mouth.

'Give us your glass.' Her voice was flat.

I handed her my half-glass of Tropicana. 'All I meant was, my dad and your mum – it's gross, innit?' I covered desperately. 'Like, the thought of the sadults having sex –'

'Yeah.' She poured carefully, leaving just an inch of clear glass at the top.

'And my mum – well, I suppose in the back of my mind,' I gabbled, 'I think she'll come back –'

Sugar snorted, handing me the glass. 'You wanna get RIGHT over that one, for starters. Once they've gone, they don't NEVER come back, parents. Even when they're right there across the table, stuffing their face and telling you you can't go on the school trip cos you're rubbish and anyway THEY never did and it never hurt them.' She narrowed her eyes nastily at me and took a huge hit of her own drink. 'Course you wouldn't know about that. But you get my drift. They go once, they're gonna go again. They're just waiting for the right ride to come along. It's not a home to them any more, it's a service station. Believe it, and get over it.'

I must have looked glum, because she suddenly decided to stop being offended and patted the bed next to her. 'Come 'ere. 'S OK.' I went and sat next to her and she reached across to the radio and turned on a dance station.

Some ecstatic-sounding dancing queen could feel your hands, your lips, the heat of your body. Well, wasn't SHE the lucky one. All I could feel was slightly sick and dizzy from bolting my drink and blotting my copybook.

She sloshed more vodka in. 'There you go. Take your med'cine.' She led by example, then lay back on the bed. 'WOoh. That's better.'

Better! I swallowed hard and silently begged to differ. I looked away, but it was too late; her blue chemise had slipped back over her caramel thighs.

I swallowed again and turned towards her; I was going to kiss her now, kiss her properly as revenge for all the teasing times she'd done it, at parties and in parks, to get some boy's attention or to get my goat. Well, I was going to kiss her good and proper this time and I knew one thing for sure – once I'd kissed her, she'd STAY kissed!

My problem was solved by Sugar sitting up quickly and announcing 'I'm gonna chuck!' before hurtling off the bed and hopscotching into the bathroom. The blood-curdling repertoire of yowls, retches and expulsions proved her to be as good as her word, and it says a lot for the depth of my feelings that I too didn't want to chuck when she emerged from my swelegant en suite, wiping her mouth with the back of her hand and exclaiming, 'Think I got a bit in my hair! Why din't you come and hold it back for me?'

I made a snooty moue of disdain. 'Really, Miss Sweet! Please remember where you are . . .'

'Oh right, no one gets sick in their wig in Preston

84

Park, do they?' She peered into my dressing-table mirror, examining strands of her silky pelt. 'Where I come from course that's the sign of a true friend. Holds your hair back when you're puking AND then lets you use her lipgloss without so much as a peep!' My disgustingly prissy outlook on personal hygiene must have shown on my face because she added slyly, ''Ere, I forgot my toothbrush – lend us yours.'

She was back in that bathroom like greased lightning inspired by evil genius and grabbing my gorgeous new battery-powered peg-polisher off the shelf before I could stop her. Waving it over my head, laughing at my lack of height and excess of scruples, she laughed triumphantly. 'Ooh, you mean you don't like the idea of my slime-encrusted gnashers polluting your lovely new toy, Kimmy? Won't Mummy buy her little princess a new one?'

I'm sure she didn't mean to hurt me, she was just used to thinking of a mother as the only functioning parent a kid has, because when she saw the look on my face – thankfully I didn't see it, as I'm certain it was vilely baby-ish and tragic – she stepped towards me, holding out her arms, still holding that sodding toothbrush. 'Oh, eff it, Kim, I'm so bloody stupid. I'm SO, SO effing sorry. And you were just talking about wanting her to come back and all –'

I wanted to let her pull me into her arms, her lovely long vanilla-smelling arms, but I didn't want it like this, me the pitied little crybaby needing comforting. So I backed away into the bedroom, shaking my head sulkily, which looking back probably wasn't too cutting edge or glamorous either. 'I want a drink.'

This was a language she understood; Sugar swooped on her backpack and got the Smirnoff out. She poured us both a couple of inches, which we drained neat in one shot, and then chucked the empty bottle at my wicker bin – a slam dunk, natch.

For the first time, and I should have recognized this as a warning sign, I felt really sad, sick at heart even, that the booze had run out. In the past, when I'd drunk with Zoe sparingly or Sugar copiously, it was something I'd done to keep them company, or at the most to 'celebrate the moment' if you want to be all rich-roast-coffee-advert about it. But now, fuelled by this weird combination of loss (Stella) and lust (Sugar), I was becoming a real proper drinker. I was drinking to forget and drinking to remember, then when I'd sunk enough I was planning to stand back and let the two of them, memory and desire, bash seven bells out of each other.

I became aware of Maria looking at me quizzically as we stood there, and I became suddenly aware of what a maudlin misery I must look, swaying stuporously as I played word games in my head. What a dainty dish to set before the Queen of Ravendene, who admired the ability to hold one's drink as much as she admired Kylie's bum or a steady hand at shoplifting. I was going to have to tough it out.

'I wan' more drink,' I pouted.

Her face lifted, her smiled socked me, and her hand

snaked into her bag and pulled out the plum, two plums, or rather two bunches of grapes alchemized into champagne and done up in dinky little half-size bottles.

'Jeez, Mareez! Where d'you get that?'

She smirked, bouncing back on to my bed and pulling me down with her with the hand that wasn't holding her fizzy prize. 'My mum's mate Shell works at the Grand, doing the rooms. My mum helped her out last week with a bunch of babysitting and on Saturday night she turns up at ours with a whole box of them as a thank you. Mum started knocking 'em back then and there and I could see that there wasn't gonna be none left for poor Sugar if I didn't take positive action. So when she asked me for the painkillers after necking three bottles, I slipped her one paracetamol and one Nytol – she was out before she'd finished the fourth one. So then, I grabbed these two and hid 'em under my winter clothes in my wardrobe and of course she don't have a clue how many should have been left next day!' She chuckled admiringly at her antics. 'Majestic or what?'

'Excellent.' I took one from her and held it to my face. 'Not very cold though, is it?'

'Ooh, sorry, Jamie Oliver, it's been sitting in my bag in the sun all day, innit, you raw prawn?' She snatched it back protectively. 'Be a good girl, nip downstairs and get some ice for it.'

'I don't think you're supposed to put the ice IN it, Shug!'

'OK, fancy-pants, we won't put the ice in it. We'll put

it down your jim-jams instead and see how you like that . . .'

She rose threateningly and I giggled, pushed her back on to the stairs and scooted downstairs to get the ice. I could hear a man's excited voice trying to whip up enthusiasm for something sporting, and my heart hurt for a moment, like someone had pinged it with an elastic band, as I imagined Dad and Matt sitting stoically watching it, two men alone, trying to pretend they liked it better that way. That being left in peace to watch a bunch of other men chasing some ball or driving some car really was preferable to having Stella swooping in and out of the room bringing drinks and nibbles and aggravation and fun and repeatedly demanding that they, 'Turn off that tragic homoerotic displacement activity and let's watch *Corrie*. PLEASE!'

Was it hell.

I shook the sorrow off me and grabbed an ice tray from the freezer. I opened the cupboard where we kept the glasses to take two proper champagne ones and was amazed to find there were none any more. But that delicate collection of eight had been Stella's pride and joy – then, with a sick lurch of my stomach, I realized that Dad must have got rid of them after she'd gone; he'd always hated her habit of opening a bottle of champagne at the flimsiest pretext, claiming probably correctly that you couldn't cultivate a champagne lifestyle on a real-ale budget. ('Oh, for Chrissake, Nathan, take that poker out of your ass and loosen up a little, can't you – it's called "disposable income" because you're MEANT to fritter it away. If you were meant to save that part of your money for a rainy day, it'd be called "rainy-day income", savvy?') But I bet he wished he hadn't now . . .

Stupidly, more than anything big, this made every-thing seem so lost and final; I felt a lump in my throat and willed tears to wash it away, but none came. Finally I turned on the taps and hung there over the sink, and my tear ducts opened up in sympathy. Only took three minutes and I felt much better, splashing my face with cold water to hide the hideous stains of emotions from the cool, hard eyes of Sugar.

Back in the bedroom Maria was wrestling with a cork. 'Stand back, Kimmy, or you'll never play the nose-flute again!' It ricocheted wildly across the room, bouncing off the door, which I only just in time dodged behind. I re-entered the room to find spume spilling all over my tasteful beige carpet and a dirty, beautiful girl sucking greedily at the bottle.

'Shug!' I complained, shutting the door behind me. 'Pig! – DON'T do that! Not after chucking up! I'm not drinking anything out of that bottle.'

She took it away from her lips and regarded me with some amusement. 'But, Kimmy, you'll let me snog you when it suits you – and you certainly don't know where my tongue's been.' She burped. 'Neither do I, come to that! Don't worry, I'll open this other one too and we can have one each.'

She started wrestling with the second cork.

Blushing hotly I busied myself collecting our vodka glasses and rinsing them in the bathroom. I heard another pop and when I came out Sugar sprang six ice cubes from their tray and dropped three in each glass; the champagne was poured very pointedly from separate bottles and we raised them in a toast.

'To friends,' I said, and, 'To having it large, loads of it, all the time,' she said, at the same time. We gaped and giggled.

'All right, to friends having it large, loads of it, all the time,' she decided, and we clinked again. Then I took a sip of my drink and Maria a huge belt of hers.

She screwed up her face. 'Jesus . . . ain't exactly a Bacardi Breezer, is it? Sour as shit.' She studied the label. 'Billencourt Salmon.' She sniggered. 'Sounds a bit fishy to me! You sure it's not off?'

I groaned and fell on to the bed. 'Shuuug! It's MEANT to be like that. It's dry –'

'It seemed pretty wet when it was soaking your lovely rug, sweetheart!'

'Champagne's prized for its dryness. It's an acquired taste.'

'What's that when it's in?'

'Like . . . I don't know, olives. Oysters. Something that you've got to sort of TEACH yourself to like, and you can only do that by keeping on doing it, over and over again.'

She looked at me disbelievingly. 'You're 'aving a laugh, aren't you? Why on earth would a person put themselves through that? Like you're trying to punish or blackmail or lie to yourself!' She shrugged. 'Whatever. Life's too short.' She grinned. 'Nip downstairs again, babe, and get us a bit of sugar to put in it.'

'You can't put sugar in champagne! It'll make it worse!'

'Baby, ain't NUTHIN' that can't be improved by a little sugar in it . . .'

Nevertheless, she drained her glass and sank back upon the bed again; again I turned my face away to avoid her thighs and beyond. Then she sighed loudly. 'It was good today, wunnit?'

I nodded and drank my champagne. It had been the most brilliant day, and the way I can explain it best is to say it had somehow been like a music video. I read in the paper that Winona Ryder said she wanted life to be like a 'movie', that she expected credits to roll when she woke up in the morning and incidental music to play when she walked down the street. This was meant to be really shocking and modern and edgy, but I thought it sounded dead corny and boring. I mean, films are so long and for so much of the time nothing happens! Me, I always wanted life to be like a video, and with Maria somehow it always was; running, laughing, taunting, teasing, and always to the thump-thump-thump of soaring, searing dance music.

We had seemed to be sprinkled with fairy dust or something as we sashayed and shimmied and shimmered from pier to arcade to seafront cafe-bar and finally to Saltdean Lido, the finest open-air bathing spot on the South Coast.

Settling ourselves on a pair of Union Jack towels with

the basic necessities – chips, Cokes, packet of Marlboro Lites, lighter, attitude – I don't think I'm too far up myself if I say we must've looked like a pair of models out of the teen magazines; Maria the colour of crème caramel in a white cozzie, long and lush with her long, dark hair flowing over her tanned shoulders, and me the colour of, well, slightly rancid crème fraiche I suppose, compact and curvy with my blonde hair turned into a regular old golden crown by the sun. We sat there, just smiling at each other, shimmied to a standstill, thinking about all the boys who had wanted us that day, and how none of them had got us, not for a minute; how we'd let them pay for drinks and rides and candyfloss and then run away laughing, their cries of 'Slags!' and 'Bitches!' ringing in our ears like respect rather than derision.

You can do that when you feel really strong, I was discovering – alchemize trash into treasure, abuse into applause.

When you felt strong, and when you had a brilliant friend. I wondered if I dared to stroke her hair . . .

'Dean Craddock!' She sat up straight, propelled by the force of her amazing breakthrough. 'That was his name! Last bloke I let finger me! Last Saturday night. I was TRY-ING to remember his name all week and I couldn't and it made me feel really nasty! I feel better now I know it again. Mind you,' she added gloomily, 'I don't remember what we done after that, so come to think of it I feel nastier than ever now . . . Kimmy, you don't think I'm a slag, do you?'

What's more important, love or truth? Can you have

one without the other? Or maybe they can never, ever coexist? Sad, innit – other girls have sex or dive off the Palace Pier when they're drunk, I conduct philosophical debates with myself.

'No . . . well . . .' I faltered. 'I mean, I don't even know what you DO . . .'

'I know.' She laughed. 'It would probably help a bit if I could actually remember what I DO with boys when I'm off my face, wunnit . . .' She rolled over on the bed, clutching a pillow to her stomach. 'Would help if I could actually remember whether I LIKE it or not! – and if I din't like it, would that make me more of a slag or less of one?'

'Decisions, decisions,' I mocked her gently. She thumped me hard on the arm; it felt like a caress.

'An acquired taste, I s'pose,' she murmured, 'like olives, innit – sex. Think about it. Boys and girls – we all like the same stuff usually; ice cream and booze and fags. We all know what's nice and what's yucky. But then, suddenly, when it comes to SEX, if you're a GIRL you're suddenly meant to like something which any boy would find really nasty if it happened to him – having a great sweaty thing bouncing away on top of you, and after five minutes he squirts all this stuff inside you! Don't sound so tempting when you describe it in the cold light of day, does it! – no wonder we've got to get pissed to let them do it to us. Ain't none of them would fancy having that done to them –' She burped loudly. ''Cept if you're GAY.' Her gaze fell on me, and her hard face softened – but not a lot.

''Ere, Kimmy – you're not gay, are you? You never mention any blokes you fancy.'

'Get lost!'

'Only if you are, I'm not dissing you. You're pretty, so it's not creepy – not sad. I'm just curious, is all . . .' She reached over and grabbed drunkenly at the toothbrush on the night table. ''Ere . . . you think they use these on one another?'

'Who?' Someone had poured superglue down my throat when I wasn't looking and I could barely speak.

'Lesbos. Dykes.' She turned it on and ran it down her thigh, but it was me who shivered. 'It's like a vibrator, innit . . .'

'I don't know,' piped the odd woodland chipmunk who had taken possession of my all-too-human body.

'Course it must be! – cos it, it, VIBRATES,' she concluded weakly. Well, I never said I loved her for her reasoning capacity. Hell, she's friends with ME, so how good can her judgement be?

Then she rolled right across till she was next to me, looking up with a smile so devilish that if she'd have had a moustache, she'd have twirled it. 'We could always try it . . .'

'What d'you mean?' I swear my heart stopped.

'Like they do. When they're gay.' She ran the brush, still buzzing, along my leg. 'Always a first time . . . for an acquired taste . . .'

'I've got to – wash my face!' I squealed, and sought sanctuary in the bathroom. For the first twenty seconds, sensible, squeaky-clean little Kimmy was in control, and planned to stay locked in there all night, safe from harm and sexual high jinks with the most beautiful girl in Brighton (THE WORLD!) – but then go-to-hell Kizza, sidekick royale to the Queen of Ravendene, kicked the wuss to the kerb and took over, and I was swishing toothpaste around my mouth, biting my lips and pulling down my jim-jams. To hell with it – let me at her!

I threw open the door and stood there proudly, five foot three of sheer blonde, teen sex.

And threw myself on to my futon in disgust as Sugar slept on, snoring like a pig in muck.

9

By the way, I don't want you to think that my entire waking hours were spent mooning after Maria, getting so drunk I couldn't remember my postcode and getting better acquainted with my toothbrush; no, no matter how sordid and/or exciting my new life as a Raver was proving to be, I still had fifteen solid years of the middle-class work ethic behind me, and so a nice juicy project – Miss Parsons's challenge to create an alternative universe through the medium of four of its inhabitants – was heaven for the good little girl I really am. Most nights when sober, which increasingly meant nights when I was hung over from drinking with Sugar the night before, I could be found huddled over my computer, gazing at it with such rapture that you'd have thought it WAS Maria.

There's nothing like a nice bit of homework to give a girl an excuse to stay up in her room all evening long, bar a brief appearance for dinner, and with the way things were going on Planet Lewis this was no minor consideration. We'd got over the savage, stunned, shock phase of Stella doing a runner, when every cuddly TV commercial featuring a warm, wise-cracking family revolving around a playful, pretty mother (ours had been a bit TOO playful and pretty, as it turned out) made Matt and me collectively wince as though a mild electric current had been passed through us, and made Dad suddenly remember that he wanted to see something on BBC2. One day early on I came in and found Matt crying in the kitchen as 'Mama' played on the radio; I flicked it off so hard I broke the switch, and hugged him, and had yet another reason to hate the stinking old Spice Girls. Were they the first group to always seem like a really half-arsed 'tribute' band of themselves, or what!

But that was then and this was now, and things were different – calmer, yeah, but a coma's calm too, so does it HAVE to be a good thing? We'd healed, it seemed, but Stella was still a scar, a livid scar, and the calm was eerier in a way, more definite, more permanent. Before it seemed like there'd been a row – things were upset, unsettled, and might still conceivably be put right, put back as they were. Now, as the weeks went by, this new arrangement, this new amputated family (much more descriptive than broken home, which sounds quite exciting – this was just a dull ache where Stella had been), became gradually normal, and we regrouped accordingly. Except I just didn't want to be downstairs, with Dad and Matt, for one minute longer than I had to.

Anyhows, I don't want this to turn into some sort of whining Yank TV nag-fest, like, 'I saw Mommy kissing Santa Claus when I was six, and now I'm a serial killer!' I look at it like, Stella grew up in a totally loving, faithful family, and it didn't stop her from turning out to be a runaway mother; I'm growing up in a 'broken' home and equally it doesn't mean I'll end up abandoning my husband and two veg for a man so young he only shaves once a week and so rich he only lives in England once a year. Parents can't just STOP LIVING once they have children, cut off their emotions and, yuck, sex organs and everything else and pretend to be nothing more than walking, talking, incubating units there to raise their kids. I'd rather Stella ran off with Blue, all of them, than stuck around here being a cow out of some weird idea of sacrifice. Because OF COURSE then I'd know it was because of me, and I'd feel guilty that she wasn't happy. More than anything I want her to be happy.

Ooh . . . look at that then! Frea-ky! When exactly did it become the norm that KIDS bring up their parents. That WE worry about THEIR happiness? Like, 'All you can do is bring them up – you can't live their lives for them!' It was meant to be the other way around, surely. Well, we're here and we can't get back to base; there's a crazy on the plane and nowhere to land. So best go on and not NAG about it – like, 'My mum made me a junkie – my mum made me a drag queen!'

Right now, I just don't want to be downstairs, that's all. I stopped believing in ghosts of dead people when I was about five – they don't frighten me. It's the other sort I can't stand now I'm growing up – anti-ghosts, un-ghosts, that awful void caused by living people who've chosen to leave you behind. Believe me, I'd welcome a poltergeist with open arms, no matter how mischievous, if he'd drive out Stella's absence. At least then we could see the damage that was being done, and we could tidy it up, put everything back in the right place . . .

Screw it, I want a drink –

I shake myself impatiently and frown at the screen. All my life, school-life, for as long as I can remember, I've been able to use homework as a way to escape the difficult bit, the emotions bit, the life bit. When I didn't fancy boys like other girls; when I grew tits before other girls; when I didn't grow tall like other girls; when I couldn't come out with the smooth spiel like other girls, acting like the star of my own talk show with everyone from flashers to other people's grandmothers, I could be top of the heap in this other world, get points in this other game that would one day put me ahead of the confident crowd. But now – whether it was growing up, losing Stella, meeting Maria, drinking, smoking puff – I just couldn't see the point any more. WHY would I want to do well at school? I laughed out loud at the idea.

Forget WANT, I NEED a drink. I want to forget, need to forget what I've just discovered. As I move soundlessly down the stairs, like a grave little ghost myself, the ghost of Kimmy Past perhaps, and into the kitchen where the drinks cupboard stays untroubled now Stella's gone, I realize two things, one after another, that quite shock me.

One, that at the age of fifteen I already can't, ever again, contemplate life without the solace of drink; not that I have to have it every day, mind you, just that it's gentle on my mind, grounding me, always a last-resort safety net. And two, that I don't mind this fact at all. Au contraire! I giggle as I close my bedroom door.

I'm a sadult!

I've arrived.

Well, I'm a tiny bit ashamed and also extremely pleased to report that it was JUST like putting petrol in a car – fill her up and watch her go! Half a glass of whisky – it was the first thing I grabbed and, OK, admittedly it was a long glass – and my fingers were skittering over those computer keys like a cartoon kitten on a piano. In a flash I realized how lumpen and dull the fictional world I'd been labouring over was – some dumb place where parents and their children actually told each other the truth – and so in a flash it was wiped, and the bare bones of a new kingdom laid down.

It all came together that night, a fast-forward first for slowly-surely me. My mind leaped and bounded like a bucking bronco, and I was both rider and ridden, driver and driven, cause and effect, creator and art. And when I finished, I just passed out, fully clothed, still at my desk. A year ago that would have appalled me, but now I reckoned it was, as Polly Hobart might have said, bless her, 'da bomb'.

'I don't wanna live,' moaned Maria as I opened the door next morning. She looked her usual beautiful self, but somehow gave the impression that all her different bits were stuff laid out at a car-boot sale, which she had no chance of selling and no inclination to promote, but for some reason couldn't pack up and take home. 'I'm never gonna do it again, for real this time.'

I raised an eyebrow as I closed the door and stepped out into the sun, feeling smug about my moderate drinking and its maximum result. I was used to hearing about Sugar's midnight capers by now – I'd even stopped thinking, automatically, ON A SCHOOL NIGHT!, which I thought was proof that I was pretty damn cool these days – but I still felt a sort of fleeting TWANG! like I had a tiny harp in my heart when she referred in any way, however derisory, to being out the night before. Her selective amnesia made it worse – had she Done It? Did she know yet? I smiled bravely and decided to draw a veil over the sordid details, even supposing she had any. We walked in silence for a bit then she said, 'Kizzy, you done your project? That made-up world thing?'

'Alternative reality, yes,' I said primly, hugging the candy-striped folder tighter against my chest.

'Lessee!' She grabbed at it but her reflexes were shot and I dodged her easily.

'Ma-RIA! Leave it! There's no point, anyway! You had three weeks to do this – and besides, it's not maths. We can't turn up with the same alternative reality. Be a bit of a coincidence – I know Parsons is dozy, but even she might sense something slinky.'

'Ooh, stick you!' she pouted. 'As it happens, I don't NEED to copy your poxing project. I got my own. I'm just interested. Show us!'

'NOoo!'

We walked to Preston High like that – niggling and bickering and bitching. It's a pretty obvious thing to say, but if you observe like ninety-nine out of a hundred pairs of teenage best friends you'll find them spending most of their public time together like that. Why is it? – is it because we don't want people to accuse us of being in love, or gay, or both, or is it because, and this is quite sad too, we've seen so much of our parents niggling and bickering and bitching at each other that we think it's the grown-up way to have a relationship?

It's so different from when you're little, and you can just go up to some kiddy you like the look of and say, 'I like deer,' and, bingo, if she likes deer too you've hit the jackpot and you'll be really solid for the next five years. And then the hormones hit and suddenly there's a domestic every day – 'Ooh, why did you tell Hannah I liked deer? You KNOW only wildebeests are cool! And now they think I'm a nerd like you!' Or, tearfully, 'You've only pretended to like deer all these years – if you REALLY did you'd get your eyebrow pierced too on Saturday, and not care what your mum said!' And in the end you just think, 'Oh sodding deer, I wish I'd never liked them. They've ruined everything!'

We were all bitched out by the time we got to the school – I was definitely thinking of Preston as 'the school' rather than 'school', which must show pretty good adjust-ment or rabid fatalism, I don't know which – and mooched into the art rooms, but even if we'd have been halfway through the knock-down drag-out fight of a lifetime we'd still have strolled in looking like two halves of the same smile because the first rule of best-friendship is SHE MAY BE A BITCH BUT SHE'S MY BITCH: YO, DON'T DISS MY BITCH!

Saint and Polly were already seated at a table for four,

and Sugar hauled me up to them; I knew better by now than to protest.

'Bags. Feet!' Maria pointed at the offending objects taking up the remaining chairs. They were sulkily removed and Maria thoughtfully offered the chair the feet had been on to me. 'So.' She gazed happily at the pair of them, who were looking at her with resigned disgust, as if she was something that had just been served for dinner three days in a row and hadn't even been acceptable the first time. 'You been gettin' down with the playas then?'

'Hardly. I went to see Coldplay,' said Zoe stiffly.

'Coldplay, eh?' Sugar nodded. 'Right. Maybe you could clear something up for me –'

'What.' It wasn't a question.

'That song – the famous one –'

'There's lots of "famous" ones, as you put it, though that's hardly what Coldplay is about –'

'Whatever. It's that one about – you KNOW – it's the one that sounds a bit dirty.'

'The one about the scientist?' offered Polly anxiously, eager to bring this tease-fest to an end.

Zoe turned to her. 'What's dirty about being a scientist?'

'Well – he could have been doing sexy experiments or something. Sexperiments, know wha' mean!' Polly opened her mouth to laugh, then thought better of it.

'Well spotted, Po-Ho!' said Maria sweetly. Then she zeroed in for the kill. 'I know – "Yellow". Thassit!'

'What's dirty about a colour?' Saint had obviously done

103

the maths and decided that bringing this silliness to a quick end was preferable to ignoring it and letting it drag on.

'Well – not if it was just a bunch of bananas he was singing about. Or lemons. But he keeps going, "And it was all yellow!" – with that sort of little weird smile. So like –' Maria twinkled at Zoe – 'is he some sort of perve that gets his kicks from weeing on everything, or what?'

Polly half-laughed, then smothered it as Saint shot daggers at her. 'You're tragic, you know that?' she told a chortling Sugar.

'And when he's apologizing, right, that he never meant to cause you trouble? It's cos he did it all over your homework, the dirty dog, and now you got detention. Cos it was all YELLOW!'

I sighed wearily. Sugar was on a hiding to nowhere with this one. A Raver girl might well intimidate a Pressie with a sophisticated sex joke, but finding bodily elimination funny put you on a par with the first years.

I was relieved when Miss Parsons ambled in. And then I remembered my art project, and I was pleased. Very, very pleased. I bided my time, like the star I was. And out of character as it was, I sneered inwardly at the competition.

I decided that Polly Hobart's quite cringingly clichéd paradise, 'OneLoveLand' – where everything was 'sweet' and 'sorted' and every citizen was the colour of a Classic Toffo – made one almost wish for racial strife. Maria Sweet's almost criminally unimaginatively named, and appallingly illustrated, 'SweetWorld' was predictably direct in its daft self-gratification – a weird version of the Big Rock Candy

Mountain. Except here there were no soda-water fountains and lemonade springs, but rather – and I quote Miss Sweet – 'the rain's made of vodka, right, so all you got to do is lean back and open your mouth to get caned, and the cheese is made of Cheestrings so it don't ming – and the grass is made of grass! WHAT?' (Blinking innocently.) 'I don't mean drugs, miss – I just mean a different sort of grass!' (Winks at class.) 'That's always green and lovely, and don't go all yellow and manky!'

Zoe Clements brought us back to earth with a bump with a vision so lacking in insight or artistic merit that it can hardly be dignified by the name; sadly, her almost legendary shortfall of tolerance and/or imagination made certain that she progressed no further – when the sky, and far beyond, was the limit! – than a tiresome obsession with literal-mindedness which rendered her 'alternative' universe depressingly censorious. 'My world is "Straightside", right, and it's a place where everyone says what they mean and means what they say. And if you don't, if you can't pull yourself together for once' – (glare; possibly at me but probably at Humankind in general) – 'and follow this very simple rule, you're going to suffer the consequences. So if you say a material possession, like a handbag, is "to die for", you're gonna die if you get it. "Raining cats and dogs" – they're gonna fall on you and you'll probably be fatally injured – at least maimed. "I went ballistic" – you'll turn into a bomb and blow yourself up.'

Seeing the many looks of dumb, appalled guilt as we each tried to recall how many clichés we used in the course of a normal day, Zoe smiled like a professional party-pooper whose job is done, and returned to her seat.

Maria was unimpressed though, not being prissy enough to care about misuse of the language of Shakespeare.

'Well, let's hope that she thinks she's as fit as a butcher's dog, as happy as a pig in muck and as free as a bird if she ever gets there. She can be her own petting zoo!' Beat; snigger. 'Probably is . . .'

It was quite funny, but I didn't laugh – I was too busy savouring my approaching triumph.

I'm not by nature up myself, but I had to hide my smirk of quiet confidence as I walked to the front of the class.

I unrolled my drawings – the best I had ever done and I've always been good at it – and carefully put them up with Blu-tack, as the others had done. Then I faced the class with the composure that comes only from giving a hundred and ten per cent and reaping the rewards.

'My alternative world is called Crap Cartoon Country – CCC for short – and it turns on its head the convention that cartoon characters have to be fun and interesting, unbound as they are by the bonds of reality. These characters are just as ordinary and unexceptional – though lovable in their own mild way – as millions of people.' There was utter silence, which I took to be awe.

I pointed at the first drawing. 'For instance, this is Tense Tiger.' I paused, then hit them with my killer punchline. 'He just CAN'T RELAX!' I waited for the roar of appreciation; but answer came there sod all. I figured that they were mute with fascination, too intent on the wondrous unwinding of my tale to interrupt with something as low as laughter. So I continued, compelled by their collective will.

'And this one – this is my favourite, Procrastinating Pig.' Pause. 'He PUTS THINGS OFF!' Silence. 'Always,' I added. Slightly spooked by the silence now, I turned back to my drawing: 'And this is Modest Moose.' My mind went as blank as the faces staring at me. What the hell did Modest Moose do, or rather not do? 'HE-NEVER-TAKES-THE-CREDIT!' I gasped. There was a lone giggle, but it wasn't a good one. Panicking I turned to my pièce de résistance. My very best picture, which I'd laboured over for hours.

'But the peace, even the benign boredom you could say, of the CCC is threatened by this dangerous maverick – Henemy. Tired of just muddling along, he seeks to overturn the established order and substitute the happy coexistence of the crap cartoon characters with cut-throat comic competition in which the spoils go to the drawing with the most obvious raison d'être and the rest can go hang.'

I stood back and waited for the response, which would surely be all the sweeter for the delay. Henemy was a fine figure of a hen, if I say so myself – drawn like the others about a foot high, wearing spurs on his feet, a Red Army-type military cap decorated with the image of an egg rather than a star, his beak twisted in a really vicious, superior scowl. You don't think of a hen being pure evil personified as a rule, or even of having a particularly expressive face, but somehow it was written all over him – he was power mad and bad to the bone.

Silence.

Then another giggle.

I pulled my ace from the hole. We'd only been asked to provide four examples, but I'd been on a total roll last night and hadn't see the point in quitting while I was ahead. I pinned up three more drawings and stood back. 'And these are Henemy's vicious henchmen – Henemy of the State, Henemy of the People and Henemy Within.'

I stood back and waited for them to laugh at my considerable wit. You could have heard a pin drop in the moments that followed. And then you could hear the pin, a big, long cartoon job the size of Henemy himself, being collectively retrieved and stuck square in the middle of my self-esteem by a shrieking, sneering roomful of banshees – Ravers and Pressies united in the delicious thrill of laughing at rather than with someone.

Someone began to cluck, and far-fetched as it sounds that clucking seemed to hold within it the purest, most searing contempt for everything I had ever been and done, everything I was, and everything I would ever be and do. And that nasty clucker was Zoe. Zoe Clements, the so-called Saint, my once best friend.

The clucking spread; the cacophony was soon so loud that it drowned out the voice of Miss Parsons as she (I imagine) first demanded and then begged for order. I stared dumbly out at the hysterical crowd, and it didn't comfort me at all that one face, even the face I loved more than any on earth, was twisted in distress and then fury.

Sugar.

As I ran from the room I was aware that she'd jumped to her feet and with the unearthly war cry I'd first heard when she rescued me from JJ, flung herself at Zoe. But all I could feel was my humiliation, which felt like an actual scalding must do, as though I'd been doused from head to toe in boiling water. Only the boiling was inside too, and it overflowed from my eyes as hot, hurtful tears.

I ran through the school gates and straight across the road; car horns blared and they sounded like the classroom laughter. Then all I could hear was the sound of my feet as I pounded on; I never dreamed I could run so fast, so fast it sounded like two pairs of feet instead of one.

I could see the trees of Preston Park before I realized that it was two pairs of feet. And then I heard her voice.

'Kim! KIMMY! Wait up!'

Instead I went faster. Because this was the worst part of all; being made to look a sad, lame fool in front of the coolest girl in the world. Even though she'd been the only one not laughing, it was her face that had hurt me most – the pity and the fury. I wasn't a proper best friend at all, to the best girl, like I'd been kidding myself; I was just another nerd with a crap home life and rubbish trainers.

I ran through the park until I was exhausted, running away from her as much as from them, and then when I could run no more I flung myself on to the grass. I was in the Scented Garden, and the searing perfume of the especially fragrant flowers, planted to paint themselves on the black velvet canvas of the minds of the blind, seemed to mock me for my own type of totally avoidable and shameful blindness. Henemy! What the hell had I been thinking of? Clever, clever Kimmy – the stupid bitch.

'I thought it was majestic,' said a soft voice above me. 'That effing Henemy – he was a git, but he really rocked.'

I felt her sit down beside me, and then I felt her hand on my hair, stroking it slowly and steadily. 'Tiger-Features too – he'd be a right laugh out clubbing. Bet I know why he can't relax – out his box on Charlie!'

I laughed, but not because she was making me feel better – I laughed because it so wasn't her, this mercy thing, and it made me feel embarrassed for her and I wanted her to stop and be hard, fast Sugar Sweet again. So I pretended I was cheering up, so she'd stop and be her old nasty self again, because right now I needed something that stayed the same, that never changed. But my laughter had the opposite effect, and encouraged her, and she continued to make a clown of herself, to be AS RUBBISH AS ME!

'And that Poncing Pig, he was a right good –'

'Shut up!' I turned on her, kneeling up and pulling her down by the wrists.

'Can't you stop babbling for five seconds? I just want to be alone, can't you understand that? You can't, can you? You effing people! – you POPULAR people! You can't imagine EVER wanting to be left alone, not to have loud music or shrieking or admiration drowning out that thing you're scared of, you who's meant to be scared of nothing! Well, can you?'

She didn't break away or even raise her voice. Just looked at me with the most infinite, heartbreaking kindness. 'So what am I scared of then?'

I should have stopped then but I couldn't; I couldn't stop now just as much as I couldn't start before. 'You really want to know?'

'Yeah.' It was the quietest she'd ever spoken, probably including in her sleep.

'You're scared of the fact, everyone like you's scared of the fact, that you've got nothing, NOTHING! inside, despite all the window dressing. You're scared that inside you're just as boring as all the people you laugh at and look down on. And that's why you can't stand being alone, and being quiet – because then your ordinariness, that you spend your life trying to drown out, just deafens you!' I pulled hard on her wrists for extra emphasis; I didn't care what I did any more! Our friendship was obviously completely over, so I might as well make the best of the closing act. I'd never get to love her, so hurting her (mildly of course, me being Kimmy) was the next best thing.

She just knelt there and looked at me. And I saw something change in her eyes, which had previously been so soft and sweet – the eyes of a stranger. They hardened now, they glittered and danced, and suddenly she was Sugar again. Even her voice held her harsh essence when she finally spoke, quiet though it was.

'You think I'm afraid of silence then, do you, Kizza?'

'Yes!' I stared at her defiantly, ready to be ruined, rumbled, kicked to the kerb forever.

'Well, why don't I just prove you wrong. By shutting you up.'

Her mouth was like a flower opening – like when they speed up the film on TV. As she pushed me down on to the grass, the smell of honeysuckle filled my head and I raised my face to the brazen blue sky, my day in the sun come at last.

We lay in each others arms, giggling. Then she stopped, and frowned.

'What?' I couldn't stand for her to be sorry – to regret it. To regret ME.

'Na – it sounds weird!' She smiled so guilelessly at me that I wasn't a bit scared any more. 'I was just gonna say – this sounds so weird, and I'm not trying to be funny, honest –'

'Go on.' I traced the shape of her lips with my finger.

'I just thought all of a sudden – well, that wasn't a BIT gay!' Her eyes widened in mock amazement. 'And – well, it SO should have been!'

And we started giggling again, then stopped still as a man came towards us. But as he passed by, his golden guide dog grinning at us, he smiled too.

'Play on, children,' he said.

So we did.

10

Well then, that was that and this was it – fireworks exploding against a dark, velvet sky, train speeding into a tunnel, the cork coming out of the champagne bottle; over and over – more, now, again! It was every smutty, blushing, glorious cliché in the world; it made you realize at last why the sadults wanted to keep sex to themselves.

Except this was PROPER sex, in a way that a boy and a girl our ages could never have had. It was sex without the rubbish, without the fear, without the you-made-your-bed-young-lady-and-now-you're-going-to-have-to-lie-in-it punchline; the pregnancy, abortion, disease, boy-boasting, bad rep, whatever. It was as ceaselessly gratifying as checking out your swimsuit straplines in the mirror at the end of each day in the sun and knowing that your tan gets deeper, sweeter, stronger every day.

It was like being on holiday and finding out that the holiday was actually home, and you'd never have to go back to boredom again. And it was like coming home, letting out your breath in a slow, luxurious glide after finally finding out that you'd been holding it in all your life. At last you could relax. You were only fifteen – but now, for the first time, you really were a kid, blessed and blissed out and born again.

That's the thing about sex, isn't it? We pretend it's the most grown-up thing you can do, but only to cover up the fact that it's the only way we can get back to being a BABY, of all things, just at the point when we realize that being a grown-up isn't just not all it's cracked up to be, it's nothing BUT cracked up. To be a sadult truly is that – to be cracked, shattered, fractured; never to be pure again.

I was amazed – I who had been born both dismayed and resigned; I would look up during the worst moments (double physics) feeling her looking at me and fearing that she was already bored or disgusted and instead see her habitually and haughtily blanked-out, beautiful face fizzing with puzzled pleasure. She would pop her head back slightly when I caught her eye, as if someone had clapped their hands in her face, and somehow I knew this was a good sign, even before she smiled and touched her upper front teeth with her tongue. She was well-behaved in class now; at last she wanted to pass for normal, because at last she really wasn't.

Our teachers were amazed at the new Maria Sweet, I could tell – this strange girl who no longer put bubblegum in the Bunsen burner or hair gel on the climbing ropes. They thought she was being good, but I knew she was just being bad in a different way. She was being bad just for me, and it was to me she murmured secret, sexy passwords of rebellion in each lesson whereas once she would have cheeked the teacher.

She was sweeter to the teachers, her rebellion now complete and extra-curricular, but she was far nastier to our classmates, Ravers and Pressies alike.

'Hey, Edward Scissorhands –' This to a good-natured,

pretty, adopted half-Vietnamese Raver girl, who occasionally slashed her arms slightly when it all got too much – 'You wanna get some stitches in that, your stuffing's gonna fall out!' A helpful, modest, mousey Pressie bulimic, who'd already been approached by a Select scout in the street last summer and turned down the chance to model because she didn't think she was attractive enough, was invariably treated to, as she sat down to her modest lunchtime repast, 'Oi, Stick Insect – you wanna go and chuck that straight down the bog, cut out the middle man!'

I'd look at her, despairing, adoring, as she sat back, smirking and basking in the silence that she mistook for respect but which was really a complete lack of impact on both victim and bystanders. I should have told her how silly she was there and then, how her 'empire' was rapidly becoming about as awesome as Legoland, but it made me love her all the more – that she was well on the way to being as mighty and majestic as a mini-mint – and therefore I grew more and more protective of her. In a way too I suppose I felt responsible for the diminishing of her powers; like Eve in reverse, I'd offered her the apple pie of cosy contentment, of physical fulfilment if you want to be yucky about it, and she'd swallowed it right down.

But what did I care? When we were alone, when we were naked in my single bed, or lying in the dark with our skirts up and our knickers in our handbags in Peter Pan's Playground or on the beach, life was perfect at long last – as perfect as Planet Earth before people, perfect like snow before footsteps. And I should have made the best of it, every precious sexed-up second of it, and not even wasted a moment caring about whether or not her one-liners had seen better days.

There's two things I know about love now, and the first one is that finding it and holding it isn't like building something, but rather like EXCAVATING something, finding a precious gem buried in the ground. And the second is that you've got to run really fast and never look down. Of course I wasn't able to manage either, but then I'm a) really short-sighted and b) a very slow runner. You might be able to pull it off. Don't bet on it though. Love has a way of making short-sighted stumblebums of the best of us.

But for now, it was that first perfect bit of love; when the whole world seems to consist of two hearts in a hammock, slung between the two brightest stars in the sky.

So we were lying on the beach one afternoon towards the end of the summer – the beach that stretches beyond the ruined West Pier to Hove.

Maria said I just liked that bit because no one we knew – no one young – went there, and I had more of a chance of being allowed to 'fiddle' (her word) with her in broad daylight, but she was crude like that. When it was her turn to choose, she went for the thriving, heaving stretch of shingle from the west of the Palace Pier to the end of the big hotels, where bandstand, volleyball court, water-sports centre, bungee jumping and other healthy outdoor pursuits rubbed shoulders with and, as the day wore on, succumbed to the insinuating, triumphant smell of marijuana in a way that was the essence of Brighton. This was 'Brightonitis' in action, for sure; you could almost see the city itself personified here, waking up bright and early on a beautiful day and hightailing down to the seafront DETERMINED to get high on life itself, just throwing balls and paddling boats and boinging up and down in the bungee like a big baby in its bouncer. And then, gradually, succumbing to the siren song of the stoner.

Anyway, there we were on a sunny Sunday afternoon in early September, lying on our fronts, wearing our tankinis and scrunchies and attitudes and not much else, moving our heads to the house music on my little radio and watching the starlings circling over the end of the West Pier and trying not to think about starting school next week. Like utterly, totally straight. All right, just a tiny bit stoned. But forget-your-shoe-size stoned, not forget-your-phone-number.

Maria was looking really gorgeous, tanned as dark as she could get and wearing a tangerine two-piece that made you want to just peel her and suck all the juice out till it ran down your chin, and I was feeling a bit emotional, yuck, so for once I was glad that Brighton had shingles not sand, so I wasn't tempted to pick up a handful of fine golden grains and run them through my fingers wistfully, like some cheap visual gag about IS TIME RUNNING OUT FOR OUR TWO BEAUTIFUL SEX-BEAST HEROINES?

I felt so pleased that I'd laid off the cheap metaphors

that I not only patted myself on the back mentally, I patted Maria actually. Not so much patted as rubbed, in a sort of circular movement, under her tankini top. I thought I was being sexy and European; I wasn't to know she'd react as though a gull had chosen that moment to send her a message from on high. She sat up straight, shaking off my hand, squinting from side to side to see if the dirty deed had been witnessed; it's great to feel wanted, innit?

'KI-IM! Don't! You want to get caught perving or summat?'

'Ma-RIA. It was hardly that!' I lowered my voice. 'I only touched you.'

'Exactly – as in "touching up". You're the one who's good at English. You do the maths!'

I realized with a start that since we'd been lovers she never ever touched me in public any more, and wriggled away whenever I touched her. And I realized that I so missed that best-friend non-stop tactile riot, when it's just the norm for the two of you to walk down the street as entangled as two drowning men trying to win a three-legged race. Now the touching was strictly rationed – behind closed doors, or in the dark, or in deserted places. And it was only ever with one end in mind; a wriggly, gasping epiphany. Sure I liked the new way. But I missed the old days. I tried not to show how hurt I was and lay back on my elbows, looking at the pier in what I hoped was a grown-up, philosophical way. I even chanced a careless laugh, which came out more as a victimized whinny.

'You know, the French say that in any relationship there's one who kisses and one who turns the cheek.'

She snorted – people use the word a lot, lazily, but Maria really did snort, in a sexy kind of way, when she was suspicious or contemptuous, like a high-spirited horse that would probably also be pawing the ground and rolling its eyes like a mad thing as it prepared to break some fool's arm – or in my case, heart – with one slick kick. 'Well, no wonder the FRENCH say it! It's all that garlic they eat. I'd turn the bloody cheek too if one of 'em tried to kiss me.' Her eyes narrowed. ''Less it was that Daveed. Mad, innit – I still don't know if we done it or not that night with the minging culottes.'

I know it's wet, but I really felt like crying when she said that; it felt like a mini version of the day Dad told me Stella had gone. Bereft is the word, I guess; left behind. 'Don't say that!' I bleated, REALLY attractively, I don't think.

'Why not?' She looked genuinely puzzled.

'You know! Because of – us!'

'Who?' I swear, I could see her trying to work out if this was the name of some exchange student or something; Uss from Ulan Bator!

'Us!' I hissed, jabbing myself in the chest with my right index finger then pointing at her like a prosecuting counsel, totally humiliated at being reduced to acting out this most basic of human relationship concepts through dumb show. 'You and me!'

She waited yet another beat for the punchline, then

understood. 'Oh, right! Sorted!' Then doubt crept in. 'Does THAT mean I'm not allowed to like boys?'

'THAT, as you call it, which I prefer to think of as US,' I explained with ever-shrinking serenity, 'pretty much means you shouldn't like ANYONE. Not in THAT way.'

'What way?'

'You know what way!' I lowered my voice. 'Sex-way.'

'Is that anything like Safeway, 'cept the cucumbers are bigger?' she sniggered. Honest, it was like trying to have a relationship with She-Ra and Evil-Lyn at times. Only marginally less intellectually rewarding.

'It means, Maria – and I shouldn't have to be explaining this to you as if you were differently abled or something! – that you shouldn't be FANCYING anyone, apart from me. I don't, apart from you! Can you imagine how it makes me feel, seeing you drooling all down your tits at the thought of that – that – onion pedlar!' I ended weakly.

Look what she's doing to me – I'm becoming a racist idiot! AND I argued in favour of complete European federation at the annual Preston High Citizens of Tomorrow Debate. (Walked all over Saint for once, come to think of it, whose bigoted, illogical excuse for a speech had been cobbled together with none other than MY MOTHER the previous night, over a smorgasbord of Pro Plus and Bacardi Breezers, and was called 'Better Little England than Fortress Europe: Germany 0, UK 2!' As I recall, the last line had been 'AND Hitler was a vegetarian!' accompanied by an ominous smirk and a sucking of the teeth as Saint swept back to her seat. She only picked up two per cent of the vote, but was she sorry? 'Those who cannot remember history are doomed to repeat it,' she'd shrugged pompously on hearing of her defeat. 'And apparently, according to your ma, Goebbels had no balls at all. Stands to reason them Nazis were well screwed.')

To give Maria her due, she didn't get the racist stereotype. Only because she was too thick – see that, I'm in love with a girl TOO THICK to even be a racist! 'What onions?'

'Look!' I was trying really hard to keep the noise down, but goodness knows she made it hard. 'Are we TOGETHER – you know! – or AREN'T WE?'

'Well, yeah.' She looked puzzled. 'When we're – TOGETHER, you know, well, obviously – we're TOGETHER then.' She brightened up. 'But say I got a favourite CD – a single. Can I only EVER play that single, because it's my favourite? Can't I ever play another single – or,' she elaborated, obviously getting the hang of the argument, 'not even PLAY it, say, cos that implies, you know, DOING IT, but more to the point can't I ever HUM another song? Can't I have it as my mobile tone? Can't I be happy when it comes on the radio and go "Oh, I really love that song!"' She looked thoughtful. 'Or better still, say I got this favourite pair of shoes – suedette, wedges, say, quite strappy, that browny-pink colour called "Dragee" –'

I'd had enough of this; I saw my potential lives as a chocolate centre in a box of Milk Tray, a pot of lipgloss in a make-up bag and even a favoured thong in a knicker drawer flash before me and decided to call a halt to this soft parade of comparisons. Maria was musical in every way, and the best way was what made her the greatest dancer I'd ever seen – she almost seemed to BECOME the music she was moving to – but the worst way was that when she was trying to make her case about something via the medium of speech, she could descend into this endless free-association riff. We'd been there before and, love her madly as I did, I wasn't about to lose my Citizen of Tomorrow crown to a girl who thought – and I swear this is true – that irony was the way a certain metal felt to the touch, on a par with steely and silvery. I mean, come ON.

So I decided to cut her off with another bit of Continental way-of-the-world wisdom; 'Well, you know what the Italians say –'

'What?' She looked from side to side, lowered her voice. 'It's not dirty, is it?'

'NOoo!' I reined myself in and tried to radiate cool. 'What the Italians say is –' and here I smirked – '"An odd shoe fits an odd foot."'

I thought she might like it, because she liked shoes. But she didn't. She looked at me as though I'd shoved a dead seagull down her tankini bottoms and then she exploded – 'I'm not no bloody odd SHOE!' She actually risked non-essential physical contact here and shoved me hard in the shoulder. 'Sod off and be odd by yourself!'

'That's what you want, isn't it?' I yelled. 'For me to be by myself, to all intents and purposes! Why can't we ever touch? It's bloody Brighton for God's sake! It's full of gay couples –'

''Xactly!' She caught me by the wrist. 'COUPLES! You didn't say gay people there, did you, you said COUPLES! And that's what I don't wanna be – a gay, rotten, boring old COUPLE! Of any kind! Boy-girl, girl-girl, girl-goat – you name it, I ain't down on the door! And I DON'T want a Plus One!'

I was almost in tears now. 'How can it be boring, being a couple, if it's girls and we're in love . . . that's not like being a boring straight couple, that's not gay –'

'Kim. Kizzy.' She shook me. 'It IS boring. There's not just one way of being boring, you know! You can be a boring couple of blokes, a boring pair of birds – in Brighton you can see this better than anywhere! People who thought that all they had to do to stop being boring was have it off with someone that looked like them – but think about it, that's about the most boring thing you can do! Like being white and saying, "Right, I'll never get off with someone black!"'

She laughed with real amusement and spread her hands, palms up. 'What's so incredibly interesting about deciding to stick to your own kind? It's just as boring as going for the opposite side because you've been told that's normal. It's ALL boring, sex stuff, when people just use it to glue themselves together cos they feel too rubbish by themselves. Unless you MAKE it something else, just for you two, each time, something new.' She stopped and thought. 'Mind you, if a person was a hermaphrodite, I s'pose THAT wouldn't be boring even in a couple. Dead embarrassing when you're changing for games, but not boring.'

'Is that what you want me to be?' I was crying, laughing. 'A bloody HERMAPHRODITE, that can go off and – and SCREW itself, so you don't have to bother?'

'What?' She batted her eyelashes innocently. 'Who said anything about not screwing you? I'm more than happy to screw you, Kimbo. I just don't want to settle down in a little house on the prairie with you.' She stood up and put out her hand to me. 'Come on – Suzy's at work and the twins-of-evil are having their blood changed.' She hauled me to my feet and licked me quickly on my right ear. 'Let's cut to the chase – your face or mine?'

11

Well, she kissed it better – and better, and better. But by the time the sun had gone down we were queuing up outside the Brighton Centre, on the seafront, undressed to impress. Fittingly, it was the annual underage SAAD disco – Sussex Action Against Drugs, organized by an eclectic committee of local police, social-service bigwigs, nightclub entrepreneurs and licensees. There were about 300 of us hopefully germ-free adolescents, aged between fourteen and seventeen, and at a conservative estimate I'd say that half the kids I'd seen already were flying on something a good bit stronger than Lucozade Sport.

Maria sort of wore a skintight silver mini tube dress, like someone had cut the end off a condom and dipped it first in Superglue and then in sequins. With her tan and her tallness and her beautiful tits it looked pretty gorgeous in a staggeringly obvious Get Her! kind of way, but it was SO cheap that even though this was its first outing and it had never been washed, sequins were coming off with every move she made. Annoyingly, I was wearing a short black linen shift dress, and the twenty otherwise highly pleasurable minutes I had spent pressed up against her on the bus down from Ravendene had resulted in my entire left side being covered in the rotten things. Typically, when I had drawn her attention to the desecration of my understated chic, she had given me a rude shove and accused me of 'thieving'!

It had been a warning sign of imminent disaster, I thought sulkily as we stood in line. And what a dumb thing to want to come to anyway! – a dry teenage disco with free softies and a brief PA by a local boy band out to promote their first single. It SO wasn't what I thought of as being 'us'. But Maria looked plenty pleased as she turned and twisted and preened and peered, so maybe she'd been right to act surprised on the beach when I raised the issue of the obviously grotesque and imaginary two-headed beast I foolishly thought of as 'Us'.

That, and the rogue sequins, made me feel really mis. I must have looked it, because someone in front of me shook me gently by the shoulder and said the immortal words, 'Cheer up, babe – it might never happen!'

It was a boy – wouldn't you know it! Like rats, we're never more than six feet away from one, apparently. Still, it was a pretty boy – as blond as me and almost as short, poor bastard. That was going to get him some grief when he grew up, or rather didn't. A quick glance confirmed that, like me, he had the proverbial tall, dark and handsome friend, really REALLY good-looking as only mixed-race teenage boys can be, in my admittedly narrow experience. He was looking at Maria in a frank, totally unlecherous way for a change – not the way most males between the ages of nine and ninety looked at her, like a weight-watcher sizing up a Black Forest gateau. No, he was looking at her like she was – INTERESTING is the only way I can put it. Like a beautiful rare stamp or something. Yet it wasn't awe at all. There was something – I don't know – practical, critical about the way he looked at her.

'What I'm scared of is it never happening that I get a drink in this sodding crèche or whatever,' I scowled.

Blondie smiled and handed me his can of Tango; Beautiful clicked his tongue against his teeth as I took it and drank. The demonic disinfectant taste of vodka hit the back of my throat and I handed it back, gasping and smiling. 'Cheers!'

'Tom, and the old woman here is Mark,' said Blondie. Maria giggled and Mark smiled wryly, looking down. Then he looked up, from underneath these eyelashes you'd have sworn were false, straight into Sugar's eyes. I almost felt that look, its power and glory, like I'd taken the force of it myself, and I wasn't surprised when she took a step back, smiling shakily.

'Fuck! My FOOT!' said someone.

'Sorry,' said Sugar instantly. I looked at her sharply. She NEVER said sorry to strangers. She'd take sweets from them and snog them – but never say sorry. What was up?

'Kim, and this is Maria.'

'You want a drink, M?' Tom held the can out to her. She went to take it, caught Mark's eye and shook her head,

'I'm all right, thanks.'

Tom shrugged. 'Where d'you go?' he asked me.

'Ravendene, we both do. You?' I accepted the tainted Tango again.

'Varndean. He goes to Newman –'

'Did go. I'm going to Varndean from next week,' inter-rupted Mark.

'Sixth form?' I asked, trying to look interested. I was staring like a crack-whore at that tinny, but I couldn't help it. Alcohol made everything bearable, I'd discovered.

'Na, we're both fifteen. I'm leaving Newman because I'm a – well, other day, April really, I became a Lutheran. That's a kind of Christian?' He looked well cocky when he said that – the way you'd expect a boy his age to look when they announced that they'd been offered a trial by Man U. 'By Grace, Through Faith,' he added hastily, as though he'd forgotten the second part of his phone number then remembered it.

Tom groaned. 'Dude! Can we leave the Big Guy out of it for just one night, yeah?'

Mark laughed. 'You do what you like, man, but the Big Guy ain't ever gonna leave you out, not even for a night. He's your permanent Plus One, down for you, on the ride till the end.'

'Did they chuck you out at Newman, then, cos it's a Catholic school?' Maria asked, interested at the SLIGHTEST prospect of conflict.

'Na, they got Muslims and everything. I could have stayed out of assembly and that. It's just me – well, what I believe. You know, each to his own and that, but I weren't down with the crucifixes and all. And the priests creeping around and that. And the bling Rome got! It ain't godly, the way I see it. It ain't plain.'

'Do you go to a special church, then?' Maria asked

quietly, trying her best to sound godly and plain while wearing a dress you could have shown life-size in a photo-message. But I could tell she was imagining herself with her tiny ankles on his big shoulders even as she spoke.

Tom snorted. 'Yeah, it's great – it's got a duvet for a roof and a mattress for a pew. It's called his bed! – that's where he is, regular as clockwork, praising the Lord on his back every Sunday morning!'

Mark blushed – I swear, he blushed! It only made him sexier – like, how far down did the blush go? 'Yeah, I know it sounds bad. But the nearest church is miles away in London, and the trains are terrible on a Sunday. I'd have to get up at like six o'clock to get there! And anyway, we don't need no place of worship, Lutherans. It's a distraction, innit. From the individual's relationship with God.'

The crowd had been moving forward briskly during this impromptu alfresco theology lesson slash pick-up session, and as we got within sight of the doors Tom took a deep drink and handed the can to me. 'D'you wanna finish it?'

I nodded and swigged, then put it carefully on the ground. 'So, how many wives can you lot have then?' Maria was asking.

I noticed Tom reaching into his pocket. He took out a small blue tablet, bit it in half and swallowed one of the halves.

'Only one wife, girl!' I heard Mark exclaim. 'We don't believe in oppressing women and using them for sex and all that rubbish.'

'Oh. Right.' The bitch actually sounded disappointed! I laughed, bitterly I hoped.

'We're all equal in the sight of God. We've had women priests for years. In Sweden, right, where the Lutherans are the national church, they got girl vicars that wear short skirts and drive red sports cars! Not that those things mean anything,' he added quickly.

'Yeah, not fantastically "plain", is it, a red sports car?' I put in sourly.

'Can I have a pill?' I asked Tom. Listening to Maria sucking up to the God-squad made me feel like doing something wild. He gave me the other half and I swallowed it quickly, checking that no one was watching me.

''Ere we go!' Tom took my arm and guided me through the door. A bum-faced bouncer stamped my hand with the inky image of a pill with a cross through it and I giggled.

It got worse. 'Oh no!' I moaned as we got to the foyer and I saw the profoundly sad posters advertising the night's delights. 'It's only DJ Bangin'! It's bound to be crap.'

'He does all these underage raves. He's not so bad.' Tom pulled me forward as Sugar pulled Mark back. You'd have sworn they were working as a team. But they were merely united, wordlessly and shamelessly, in the age-old international language of Getting Off.

We followed the crowd to the very brink of the disco; the strobes were already off on one, and a girl in front of me stopped still and turned to her friend. 'Oh, FUCK. I can't, Jess. I'll have a fit!'

I tapped her on the shoulder – 'Excuse me. If you do, can I have some of what you're having?' I heard myself say.

Jess turned round and glared at me. 'Do you mind! My friend's an epileptic!'

'Coming over here, taking our jobs,' I cheeked. It was like I was possessed or something – possessed by the spirit of some dead, popular, casually offensive teenager.

'You bitch!' Jess shoved me. I laughed and Tom stepped between us. Who did the albino short-arse think he was, bloody Napoleon?

'Leave it for Mr Manners, ladies, eh? It don't become you. Sorry about your mate, Jess – Kim, walk on.' He stood back and ushered me past; I made it into a strut, sniggering. Maria, Mark in tow, bustled up to me, like a frigging MOTHER or whatever.

'Kiz, what you DOING? You wanna scrap or something?'

'Jus' standing up for myself. Like you do.'

She looked at me hard, then hustled me away from Mark with a nervous smile.

'Like I do?' she hissed. 'You wanna do what I do? I don't even wanna do what I do! I don't want to be some slapper picking catfights in clubs all my life. I'd rather do what you do – be nice. Be good.'

I laughed very rudely at that. 'As if!'

A sharp young Asian boy passing by smiled cheekily at me and said with a wink, 'That's my name, don't wear it out!' I laughed again and reached out to ruffle his hair.

He looked pleased and stopped walking. 'You comin', then?'

'Done!' I went to follow him, but Maria stopped me and glared at him.

'She's taken.'

He shrugged and passed by.

I glared at her. 'I LIKED him!'

'You don't KNOW him! What about Tim –'

'Tom!'

'See, you must like him, you even know his name!'

'I know what you're UP to!' I smirked triumphantly.

'Well, what is it, then?' She looked baffled, then genuinely interested – what a prize I'd won!

'Trying to get me off with that Tom, so you can get off with that – that – God-botherer!'

'What? . . . oh, THAT.' Her smile was like a bacon-slicer. 'It's just a phase . . .'

'It is NOT a phase, Maria!' Out of the corner of my green little eye I could see Mark and Tom casing us with mild concern, and it pleased me grimly. Go on then, let's her and me have a full-on total bitch-fight, and THEN when she's standing over me, panting and triumphant, I'll spill the beans on her – tell them what she and I get up to together – and that'll REALLY give them both something to go home and jerk off over. Not to mention totally queering her pitch, as it were, with the holy hottie. 'That religion of his, it's some whole 'nother hardcore lifestyle choice, for real! It's about the straight and narrow-minded, and frankly I don't see you showing much aptitude for either.'

132

She frowned. 'Yeah, but I like HIM, though, that founded it – no problem. We done him in History last year. Majestic, he was –'

Tom gestured at his watch and Sugar nodded impatiently at him while Mark adopted what he no doubt thought of as a transcendent expression and peered into the distance. He might have thought he looked spiritual, but I thought he looked like he'd let off and was trying to shift the blame.

'You mean in religion –'

'NO! For fuck's sake. History of course. The Yanks wouldn't let the black people have the vote, so they all marched against the White House and he was their leader, 'cept he didn't believe in violence so he got killed. The good die young!' she finished predictably.

I couldn't believe it – even after all this time, even after her thinking 'Coppelia' was a fruit juice and MC Squared was a DJ. This was the clincher. I laughed, feeling dizzy. 'Maria. Correct me – but you're thinking of MARTIN LUTHER KING, aren't you?'

'Yeah.' She smirked. 'He was a great man. Not surprised Mark belongs to his church.'

'MARTIN LUTHER KING, JUNIOR?'

'Oh – did his dad start the church, then?'

'NO!' I shrieked it, like they tell you to shriek at Juniors if a grown-up's touching you inappropriately. Everybody would have looked, if everybody except the boys, Maria and I hadn't already passed deep into the disco dark, dancing as though their GCSEs depended on it. Startled, the boys

133

looked at each other, shrugged, looked at us and gestured towards the darkness, quickly disappearing into it.

'Look what you've done now, you stupid cow!' Maria made to follow them; I grabbed her arm.

'No, Maria – NO! You're the stupid cow! YOU! You really think that the Lutheran church was founded by Martin Luther King Junior – don't you!'

'OK – his DAD, then! Jesus, Kim, what IS your problem!'

'Your shaky grasp on religious history aside, aren't you forgetting SOMETHING ELSE standing in the way of the prospect of true love with that – that – sonofabitch of a preacher man!' I knew it was silly and hysterical, but, hey, that was the language I was speaking now.

'Well, WHAT?' She looked at me with hostile curiosity, as though I'd pushed in front of her in a queue.

I started to say 'ME!' but stopped – I was sick of being this relationship-scold, always nagging on at her. It was pretty damn ageing, sounding like some horrible American chat-show pop psychologist, and not too sexy if you thought about it. It was EXACTLY the sort of talk to drive away a quicksilver bird of passage and paradise like Sugar, and I knew I had to rein it in. So instead I went for the sophisticated approach.

I needn't have bothered.

'So what about the little issue of MOI?'

'WHO?' she yelled above the music.

'MOI!' I yelled back. 'M-O-I!' As I did so a girl I used to know from the High passed by, giving me a funny look.

I could just imagine her saying to Zoe when she next saw her, 'Here, Saint, I saw your friend Kim the other night. At the SAAD Disco, with that flashy dark girl she hangs around with. Talking about the ex-president of Kenya!'

'Look, I don't have time for this, Kim. I'm here to party, not play spelling games. Go and find one of your stuck-up Pressie friends if that's what you want. Just get off my back! And the rest of me –'

And with that ominous sign-off she slipped through my grasp, slinky as a sequinned eel, and was swallowed instantly into the belly of the throbbing, finger-wagging beast that was the SAAD Disco.

Lost, I followed her.

It's horrible when you're lost, even in an enclosed space you know you'll eventually get out of. Every time I hadn't been picked for games (too short) or for gossip (too studious) or for flirting (too serious) came back to me in a kind of kaleidoscope of loneliness as I wandered around the big, dark, strobing space, spaced out on that amount of drink and E that's both too much and not enough. Everywhere I looked there were my generation's prime specimens, a multitude of shimmering tableaux demonstrating various aspects of totty heaven, living for and in the moment with an effortlessness that would have made the Dalai Lama look like a worrywart.

A gorgeous Asian girl in shocking-pink silk trousers and crop top demonstrated a classic hip-hop groove to a beautiful but clumsy black chick and her equally graceless red-haired white friend, them frowning and her laughing as they tried to copy her before the three of them gave it up and collapsed in a giggling heap, watched lustfully yet affectionately by half-a-dozen multi-hued boys. Chinese girl twins performed an impeccable hand-jive side by side, their appearances and movements so identical that kids blinked and pointed with good-natured surprise – Ooh, I'm seeing double, that E was stronger than I thought! – as they gathered to watch and whoop encouragement. A bunch of majorettes slipped some dirty R'n'B moves into their usual marching routine and were rewarded with refreshments a little harder than the SAAD committee would have liked by a fit, eager group of public schoolboys.

Amongst all this, this sick display of mental health and social harmony and physical well-being, I of course wandered lonely as a clod. A clod that plods, I reflected drunkenly.

And of course there were the bold ones already pairing off and getting better acquainted. 'Pairing off' – 'Couples' – what a low business it was, just like the animals going in two by two!

To be half of a couple, I decided, is to become half a person. Who needs it –

And then I saw her.

DJ Bangin' didn't have such bad taste in dance music and had so far delighted us with a number of acceptable urban chart singles mixed with old-skool classics. But you know the way everyone's got a cheesy slice of something they just can't leave behind – mine's that Alcazar song with

Richard Gere's tie in it – and sooner or later, when they're on a roll, they're going to get it out. Well, Mr Bangin's shameful secret was that old nineties handbag-house instrumental, 'Children' by Robert Miles – maybe you know it. He was an Italian, apparently, though you wouldn't know it by the name he chose to work under. Probably really called Roberto Milano or something. Whatever – he's a good man and I'll tell you why . . .

As the opening thump-thump-thump started up, I watched Maria dance, slowly at first, the length of her body moving smoothly, none of those flailing hippie limbs for her, her feet together and her arms by her sides, her neck and head and long swoosh of hair totally at one with the rest of her. I've tried to analyze exactly what made her such a good dancer and the best theory I've come up with is that she never confused dancing with self-expression, which every single other person who gets up and shakes their booty non-professionally does. But Maria expressed herself completely in every other area of her life; when she danced, all she wanted was to become one with the music. It was her time out, her higher ground; BECOMING MUSIC! She was doing that now. The strobes moved slowly over her silver body.

You see, this tune she was dancing to – 'Children' – was written for a reason, unlike most instrumentals. It had a message, and it's such a beautiful message it makes me cloud up just thinking about it.

In Italy apparently they've got a horrific road-deaths problem, and a load of them happen at weekends after young people have been clubbing and drinking and then they drive home. So this man, Robert Miles, was a DJ and he wanted to do something about it. So he wrote this tune, which he used to play as the last groove of the night at the clubs he was working. He'd put the lights up and play it. And maybe because it had no words, because it didn't say anything about not drinking and driving and wasn't wagging the finger, it worked for a while . . .

Maria was moving faster and faster now, all her precious silver self still totally together, the strobes raking her like searchlights, like headlights, like a lover who'd lost her, desperate to feel the balm of her shining spotlight attention on them once more. But she was lost in music –

Anyway, this tune, 'Children', reminded the young Italian ravers, no matter how trashed they were, that they were still precious to their parents – their BAMBINI. It starts off so delicately and builds up to something so tough and strong and pleasure-seeking, yet still with that sweet music-box motif at the heart of it – like a simple statement, with no judgements or lectures, that however much sex and drink and drugs you have, you're still their baby. And if you die, they're going to have to bury their baby. Anyway, apparently it worked for a while, and those Italian ravers changed their ways . . .

The strobes exploded, and Maria shuddered to a stop.

But the tune didn't work for long. And now apparently the road death rate is worse than ever . . .

'Your face!' Maria grabbed me by the hand and pulled me after her as she strutted away from the dance floor. 'Iss like you lost an E and found an Ex-Lax! Come on, let's show these Looky-Lous how a REAL player takes their ease.'

'We haven't got any,' I mumbled, misunderstanding her, but dumb with relief that we were friends again.

'What?' she laughed, as an orderly queue of alpha boys formed to offer her anything her hyperactive little heart desired.

'You said Es. Pills. We don't have any.'

She turned to me, took my chin in her hand and gave me the sweetest smile I'd received from her since before we had sex – since before she owned me.

'Well, if that sort of Es are what we want, I imagine that the chorus line here can sort us out something proper. But I actually meant 'ease' – E.A.S.E. You can kick back now, Kizzy, and wipe that mizzy little look off your face. Because SAAD by name and sad by nature this losers' love-in may be, but now it's MINE. And what's mine is yours.' She kissed me quickly on the lips, and the queue seemed to shiver and squeal and swell before pressing forward with even more hungry regard.

She twinkled at me, the little star secure in her blank universe. 'Except ME of course.'

For the next hour, Sugar and me were frantically fed and watered, rocked in the bosom of chemistry as it were, by this . . . QUEUE is the only word for it, and they weren't looking for anything as innocent as fifty per cent off soft furnishings though they certainly hoped that EVERY-THING MUST GO, preferably right off our sunstruck bodies and straight on to the beach. But of course Sugar was too slick for them, and she had her eye on a prize far more rarefied than some baggy-trousered B-boy up for a fumble. As she accepted the offerings that had cost them a whole week's pocket money, snogging me every six minutes to keep them coming, I was aware of her scoping out the crowd, looking for the only boy that didn't, wouldn't, couldn't want her.

Then suddenly Mark was there, and everything else seemed to evaporate on cue as he and Maria stared at each other. Except it wasn't JUST the usual West Side Story stuff – it wasn't the be all and end all, it wasn't what love's meant to be, just sweeping the two of you away, happy ever after. They looked at each other – everything else evaporated – THEN he did this more-in-sorrow-than-in-anger thing with his mouth, then he shrugged, towards the QUEUE – then he smiled, and saluted of all things! Then he turned and was gone. I was vaguely aware of Tom scurrying after him – gesturing, protesting, submitting, disappearing.

I looked at Maria – and then I looked again. Most people would have been taken aback by the object of their affliction seeing fit to bail out when they themselves were at their most foxy and feted, but she looked – damn, it was the major weirdest thing – she looked totally serene, and more than that she looked RESPECTFUL! She watched Mark turn his beautiful back on her and walk away, and for the first time ever that I've known her, and for the first time ever FULL STOP, I just KNEW, she simply looked respectful! I swear, it was the strangest thing you've seen in

140

your life, to see that emotion on her face – as tangible and fresh as wet sky-blue paint. For the first time in her life, a boy had walked away from her – shown her he was stronger than she was. And she loved him for it.

Suddenly I felt like the oldest girl in the world. Old – and very, very sad. 'You like him, don't you, Shug?' I said quietly.

'Yeah, I do . . . I WOULD . . . in another world . . . in a better place . . .' She swayed slightly, and her big dreamy eyes became even more manga for a moment. Then the stage lights went up and DJ Bangin' agitated his way to the front of the stage.

'Awright, Brigh'on?'

We made a sort of non-committal noise, as if we hadn't QUITE decided whether we were exactly what or where he thought we were.

'Awright, BRIGH'ON! Less give it up – less give mad love – to them local bwoys made good – WESTED!'

The four of them were so bland, so totally lacking in charisma, personality, character, whatever you want to call it that distinguishes us from the molluscs, that they seemed to barely make up one whole person between them. Instead – wearing baggy trousers and T-shirts which took a real dumb pride in misspelling FITT, HOTT, WETT and DIRTTY – they were like some sort of eight-armed, eight-legged, four-headed phantom beast, not knowing whether it had ambitions to be an octopus or a proper grown-up human. The noise they made – or rather their backing track made – left me none the wiser as to their ultimate goal.

They sang – or rather lip-synced, as though in a completely different language to judge by the gap between the words and their mouth-movements – their first (and last, as it happened) single, which was hovering limply around the bell-end of the Top Fifty and unlikely to hoist itself up any further. It rejoiced in the title of 'RU Freeky?'

The lead mollusc shuffled to the front of the stage and puckered up his lips:

RU Freeky?
And RU freeking weekly?
I'm gonna text ya
Cos I wanna sex ya
Hit me on my celly
Cos I want yo' jelly!

The most amazing feeling of depression engulfed me.

I turned to Sugar, just KNOWING she'd feel the same. But why oh why was I surprised to find that, yet again, two were not necessarily one! She'd made it pretty clear already that, united physically though we may have been on numerous occasions – almost ACCIDENTALLY, it seemed now as I thought about it! – there was definitely no US. For whereas Wested made me feel like lying down and crying over the death of Western civilization, her eyes were shining like black ice as they careered wildly over the wretched specimens disporting themselves onstage.

It was her fame thing of course – one of the most conventional and disappointing things about her. She worshipped fame, and admired famous people of any sort from felons to female impersonators to fiddle-players, but she just couldn't be ARSED, it seemed, to seek fame for anything herself. That would be a terminally uncool thing to do.

She grabbed me round the neck with both arms as 'RU Freeky?' drew to a merciful close. 'Ain't it COOL!' she yelled excitedly.

'Like Vanilla Ice,' I sneered.

She kissed me hard on the lips, less from desire than sheer molten glee at this pathetic parody of a perfect moment.

I thought it couldn't get much worse; I was wrong. 'HEEEY!' Oh please. Oh no. The lead Wested tosser was pointing at us with one hand and grabbing his knee-length crotch with the other. 'I spy LADEE-LOVERS! Spotlight on these well-fit freaks!'

The crowd cheered gamely as my world fell down. The spotlight hit Maria like an old friend and she smirked and preened with all the luxurious familiarity of an exotic fish plucked wriggling from the carpet and returned to its natural environment. Now she could breathe deeply of what she wanted – the pure addictive oxygen of attention.

'HEEEY! FOX-EEE! What's your name, babe?'

'MARIA!' she shouted, her arms still around me.

''RIA? Hey, 'Ria – your friend Blondie – you got a liquor licence for her?'

The other tossers cracked up.

'A WHAT?' yelled Sugar.

'A LI-QUOR LICENCE.' No, dumb-ass, no one gets it but me. And I SO wish I didn't. And before anyone does, I'll just – creep – off –

I had almost released myself from Sugar's grip when the lead tosser chose to enlighten 300 or so smutty-minded teenagers as to the point of his moronic patter. 'A LICK-HER LICENCE! LICK HER! HEH, HEH, HEH!'

And SHE laughed with them, my poor, glorious, stupid princess – laughed as our love, to me as precious and rare as a black rose, became a seaside postcard punchline, a worthy companion for the whoopee cushion and the plastic dog do. Amazingly, it made me love her more – a love held on a strange sad note that was stretched so tight it made me wince to even think about plucking it. I just went limp then, took the line of least resistance and languished in her strong careless arms. I barely protested as two bald bouncers hauled us up on to the stage – I may have whimpered slightly, in the manner of a young gazelle caught in a gin-trap. But a lot of good that did me, caught up in the full force of the moronic inferno that is teen hysteria.

''EY, BABE, YOU MUSTA BEEN READING SNEAK MAGAZINE!' The long-limbed sadist flung his arms around Maria, who still had her arms around Little Me – we must have looked like some sort of vile mutant family or something!

'WHY'S THAT?' simpered Sugar, if you can simper and shout at the same time. Why were they still shouting, while locked in a sweaty embrace? Was it simply because they were half-wits or was there something more sinister going on?

'COS THAT'S WHERE I DID THE INTERVIEW WHAT SAID NOTHING TURNED ME ON LIKE A BIT OF GIRL-ON-GIRL ACTION!'

The audience erupted, the lascivious lava of their laughter washing over my poleaxed pain and freezing me in an attitude of complete defeat and surrender.

'SNOG – SNOG – SNOG!' the crowd shouted. I was only vaguely aware of the face I loved more than any other looming over me in all its merciless, mindless beauty before the room spun and everything went black. I was going to die!

As I hit the floor, I reflected briefly that this was the best thing that had happened to me all night.

12

Even taking into consideration what you already know about the exquisitely painful, excruciatingly sustained practical joke which I pluckily call my 'life', and which I'm sincerely hoping to be allowed to share the punchline of any minute now so that I can go home and get on with the REAL one, what happened after the SAAD Disco fiasco was a real ratings-grabber. Of COURSE there was going to be one kiddy among the multitudes whose dad was a hack on the *Argus*, and of COURSE when he pulled up early at the Brighton Centre to pick up Sonny Jim there was the ambulance speeding away with its blissed-out blonde burden on board – i.e. me. Of course he followed it all the way to A & E at the local hospital in search of his story – leaving his offspring in the lurch, typical journo – and of course he was there in the lobby when Dad turned up dragging Matthew behind him, Dad blubbering like a baby while THE baby (he was only ten, for God's sake!) tried to comfort him.

The way Simon Shaw wrote about it the next day over three pages (with tearful snaps, thankfully none of me on my bed of shame), we were a family that Jerry Springer himself would have rejected as being too messy for mediation or even confrontation. Dad fully put the blame for my accidental overdose on Stella's absenteeism; me, I'm as numb as a snowman on coke, so I don't care, but I don't think it did Matthew any good hearing that stuff. OK, so she ran off with a boy young enough to be her waist measurement. But at least she had the decency to do the dirty quietly and not hang around long enough to conduct a masterclass on familial trauma courtesy of the local rag, without even bothering to change the names.

Of course, because it WAS the annual anti-drugs disco, sponsored by the coppers and the council and the caring professions alike, it was even more of a story. ABANDONED TEEN IN POLICE DISCO DRUG OD DASH pretty much covered all the bases; add a candid snap of Matthew crying on the steps of the hospital and a gratuitous glamour shot of Sugar ('Shocked friend Maria Sweat' – I liked that misprint!) finally forsaking all thoughts of keeping her dress on, and you've pretty much got a three-volume novel, except it's on a billboard reaching from here to Saturn, laying bare everything I most wanted to keep under my hat.

It SO sucked going back to school. As you know, all I ever wanted was a quiet life, and it was dismaying enough when Stella dumped me and Maria Sweet found me, overturning my presumed heterosexuality. I had thought the biggest hurdle I'd have to face was breaking it to the sadults that I wanted to go to my choice of university, not theirs, after I finished school. Now I was a walking, talking, teenage photo-trauma. Dad watched me like I was a pyromaniac in a pine discount shop; Matthew took to sleeping across my bedroom threshold, which was a bastard when I tripped over him on my way down to thieve a

147

nightcap and had to threaten him with losing not one female family member but two if he told.

Maria didn't answer her mobey for the rest of the holidays, as I expected – my credit had run out, and then some! – and she was nowhere to be seen in the playground that first day back. I must have looked a right orphan because Jolie French, like a beautiful blonde ostrich, picked her way over to me and leaned against the wall, staring. She stared at me, I stared at her and the whole playground stared at us.

'Y'awright?'

'Yeah, I'm great.'

'Y'don'hav'ta, y'know.'

I stared at her. 'Don't have to what?'

'Don'hav'ta'go'long'wit'Ria. Can be y'self.'

This was Jolie's thing now, since she'd first mopped up all the groupies who'd found Maria a mite too spiteful. She didn't need no peer group or best friend; she was beautiful and blank enough to waterski over all of us – now I'm in your life, now I'm out of it! – while offending none of us. Her parents were some sort of middle-class gypsies. It was very attractive, her whole take on stuff, I suppose. Very intelligent. I thought about it.

'Cheers, Jolie. But you know, I don't think there really IS yourself without your friends. Without your best friend, anyway. There's only half of you. Some sad shadow looking for its own. Its home.'

She shrugged – 'Fair'nuff' – and was about to sashay

away when a long, lawless arm sent her spinning on a downward spiral.

'Oi! Bitch!'

Jolie looked up bitterly from her lowly resting place. 'Oh, hi, 'Ria.'

''Ria my royal butt!' Sugar, shorn and tanned, stood with her hands on her narrow hips like some supermodel fishwife. 'YOU – if you don't want me to rip you a third arse – just up sticks and swivel right away!' We both watched objectively as Jolie suddenly remembered and set out for a subsequent engagement double quick.

Maria gazed down at me mistily. 'When I said I'd rip her a THIRD arse, I wasn't being bad at maths. I mean I know she's only got one really. I was just making fun and saying she's got –'

'I understand,' I assured her hurriedly. 'You don't need to draw me a diagram.' I stared at her. 'You cut your hair –' It was chin-length now, clinging to her face, just like I wanted to.

'Look, Kiz –' she said awkwardly.

'Shug, it's OK –'

'No, listen –'

'Honest, you don't have to –'

The bell rang and we looked at each other guiltily, as though it rang for us – ding ding, time up, knock out. Only one girl left standing. But which one?

Then 'Kimmy!' a sweet, sharp voice rang, and Sugar clenched her fists once more in order to defend her paltry prize. A slinky brunette walked over to us, looking at me all proprietorial. I was sure Shug was going to clock her one, 'specially when she hugged me tight and kissed me hard. But it was lucky she didn't, because the slinking minx was none other than Stella – my mother, my lost star.

'You've changed.' Stella shot a sideways look at me as we walked across the street to the seafront.

'Yeah, I'm from a one-parent family these days. We're deprived. Or is that depraved? Oops, no, that's you!'

But a bloke – get this! – a bloke had whistled approvingly at me, and the sad bitch thought it was for HER! Like, hel-LO – the state of your ovaries?

She was simpering over her shoulder and my put-down totally went over her empty head! 'Sorry, darling?'

'Forget it.' We got to the pier and I went to turn left; Stella took my arm and pulled me the other way.

'This way, Kimmy.'

'But I want to go this way.' I pointed towards the electric railway, the sad marina, the abandoned, enchanted, rubbish Peter Pan's Playground.

She frowned. 'But there's nothing there!'

'No, Stella.' I pointed towards the busy, bustling, reborn toytown between the two piers. 'THAT'S where there's nothing. It's just nothing in a noisy, up-itself way, so you don't realize it.'

'But the Artists' Quarter . . . the restaurants . . . the Indian Head Massage stall . . . the wet-fish shop . . .'

'Do you want to buy some wet fish, Stella?' I

demanded. It seemed unlikely, to say the least. She wouldn't even buy toilet paper because she thought it was vulgar! – we used to use Kleenex Boutique tissues instead.

'Well, no . . . but it's all so gorgeous . . .'

'Look!' I'd had enough; I stopped walking and caught her by the shoulder. She wriggled and pouted, glaring off to one side; it was tragic, but I had to laugh – it was TOTALLY like I was the parent and she was the child. 'You've pissed off to some sort of Fantasy Island for the best part of a year, drinking mango juice out of Lover Boy's navel or whatever – and now you won't even WALK for five minutes in the direction I want to. What sort of mother are you?'

She stared at me in horror for a moment, and then to my amazement she burst out laughing and took my arm, taking me in the direction I'd wanted to go.

'You're right, darling, I'm a monster.'

We walked along in silence for a bit and then Stella started sort of limping.

'Sorry, babes, it's my shoes – not very sensible –'

I looked down and saw the highest, strappiest, silliest pair of shoes I'd ever seen, even in a magazine – tangerine leather, with a tiny little orange on each toe. Gross! – there was actually blood running down the back of Stella's left heel where she'd obviously forced her feet into a smaller size. She hobbled to a bench and sat down while I followed, not knowing whether to carry her or kill her. I watched her while she lit up a Marlboro and shook my head when she offered me one.

'This is just mad, Stella. I shouldn't even be out of school. Especially not on the first day of term –'

'Look, you know I cleared it with your teacher. And with The Rock.' How did she know that nickname so quick? This is typical of her – a fountain of useless, youthful knowledge. She knows fifty ways to fold a sarong and not one to be a mother. I looked at her, fiddling with her foot and smoking – to be honest, she looked really common. And, for a moment, eerily like Sugar.

She looked up and grinned 'cheekily', which I found a bit sick considering the circumstances. 'By the way, The Rock wants to see you when you get back. Nothing heavy. Just a little chat about your naughty night at the adolescent orgy and the mercy-dash to hospital. What was it, E?'

I hated the way she said it, all nudge-nudge and knowing.

'Yeah. It was just a one-off though – I drank too much and lost it. I'm not any sort of problem child.'

'Yeah, I don't like E much either,' Mother Dear mused, 'not these days anyway. It's all been stepped on so much. Now in the early nineties –'

'I don't want to know, thanks.' I tapped my foot, frowning at her; I had enough problems, did I really need a drug-fiend mother as well? 'And, you know, couldn't this parent–child summit have waited until I got home today?'

'Oh, I'll be gone by then.' She was rooting in her handbag now.

'You what?'

'I'll be back in London this-after. I'm only here because Dom had to sign some stuff –'

I couldn't believe it. Then another thought struck me. 'How long have you been in London then?'

''Bout a week?' She stuck a pink Barbie plaster over her heel with a smug flourish. 'There!'

I couldn't help it – I just lost it and started crying, silently, sitting there with the sun hot on my face. It seemed so weird to be crying in the sun. But I couldn't stop it. She hadn't even come back to see me – she was just killing time while her fancy-piece took care of some paperwork. And she'd been back from the Bahamas for a week already – with London only fifty minutes away on the bloody train!

She looked at me, totally baffled, and miserable though I was I couldn't help but feel sorry for the poor cow – she genuinely didn't realize how cruel she was.

'I'm sorry, babe –' Then she brightened. 'I'm not seeing Matthew at all, if that makes you feel any better!'

I was so angry then I stopped crying at once. 'You effing WHAT? Of COURSE it doesn't make me feel any better! You evil bitch, Stella! Why the HELL aren't you seeing him? He's a little boy, for God's sake!'

'I know.' She actually bit her lip; it was her, not me, whose ambition was to live in a teenage-magazine photo-story. 'I thought it might be too upsetting for him. Especially seeing as I'm not going to ask him what I'm going to ask you –'

'And what's that? If you can borrow my Burberry

153

bikini? Would have thought Dom could have afforded to buy you a dozen before breakfast.'

She laughed – even at a time like this, she could laugh! You always think that's a good thing, being able to laugh in any circumstances, but maybe it's not – maybe it just means you're a raving nutter. 'Course not. I came here to ask you if you want to come and live with me.'

It gets better, believe me. Apparently she's not going to ask Matt to come out to Bounty-Bar Island too because, 'Despite those awful things Nathan's been saying about me, very FEW of which are true, it wouldn't be fair on him if you both left.' As if anything else she'd done recently was fair! And suddenly it's all going to be made hunky-dory by, 'One for you, one for me!' – this woman has got a six-year-old's sense of fair play, only not QUITE so sophisticated. And then, 'Matt's a boy,' (nice to see she remembered) 'and he'll soon have to learn about, you know, all that nasty stuff that happens to boys and men.' Presumably this means being abandoned by their wives and mothers.

Then she gets the photos out, all the while gesturing at the glorious, vivid vista of Brighton esplanade – 'Look at it, darling, it's just a run-down, small-minded provincial town behind all the pretty window dressing!' – and tells me how wonderful life would be on her exotic island, Eleuthera. When I complain that it sounds like a sort of female sex-organ bit, she pouts prettily and says, 'Well, it's really Harbour Island – we say Eleuthera because that's the nearest island a plane can land on – not a big nasty commercial plane, a really sweet little one. Then you have to get a ferry to Harbour Island itself – "Briland" as we call it. We sort of want to keep it a secret, because it really is the most beautiful place on earth.'

The photos look fine – apart from the half-dozen she simperingly snatches out when they pop up, showing me a good deal more about my mother's nipples and her boyfriend's arse (no visible nappy rash, surprisingly) than I would have chosen to know. The sea is that heartbreakingly beautiful bluey-green that makes every other colour in the world look like beige, and the sand is not JUST sand, always an improvement on our Sussex shingle, but PINK sand of all things. Stella's (Dom's) house is cool and white and low and just sort of HANGS OUT on the beach, and you can tell immediately that no shoes are ever worn or voices ever raised within its chilled-out walls.

But that's it, they're just PHOTOS, holiday snaps, things to be looked at and put away and gather dust while life, REAL life, is got on with. I mean, I couldn't live on the pier or in Saltdean Lido, much as I like to visit them, and it's typical of Stella's tenuous grasp on reality that she actually believes she can make a life in a place far more fantastic. It's suicide with scenery and a suntan.

'I've got to get back to school,' I said. Suddenly a telling off from The Rock seemed a lusciously banal prospect compared to this ludicrous proposal.

'I'll call you, darling! Think about it now!' She was putting the photos back in her bag, smiling, not a care in the world. When I looked round before crossing the road back into town, she was buying an ice cream from a van, and she shrieked her glee – 'For ME?' – at being given not one but two Flakes in her cone. So for Stella at least, brilliantly, irretrievably shallow as she was, this had been a very good day indeed. I walked on, not knowing whether I envied her or pitied her. But knowing for sure that, in an ideal world or even just a marginally less mad one, the idea of a child feeling either of these emotions for a parent just wouldn't arise.

'You're JOKING!'

We were behind the ironic bike sheds, having an ironic fag. At least, I was.

'No, she really did! Had the front to ask me if I wanted to go and live out there with her and His Nerdship!'

Sugar looked even more incredulous. 'And you're NOT GOING? You're JOKING!'

Was all the world mad except me? I wondered yet again. Or was I the mad one, wandering about in a dream world? Apparently I was mad because I had these things called 'attachments' to people, while these very same people thought an attachment was something you added to an email, and that they could be as easily and painlessly put in the trash, just by clicking on an icon.

I looked at Sugar, and realized that even in our relationship, vastly more experienced than me as she seemed, I had once again ended up as The Mother. As indeed I had with my own mother! I couldn't believe how me and Maria had started out – such a short time ago! – all fireworks and passion, and now more and more it was like some clenched, clammy familial relationship which gave more pain than pleasure, at least to me. I couldn't believe how much like dealing with Stella it was; like teaching her to read, slowly and laboriously, from some imaginary, illustrated Baby's First ABC of Morality: 'A is for Avarice, which Baby mustn't do/ B is for Bullying, and that's bad too –'

'But it would be BAD if I went to live in the Bahamas, wouldn't it, Sugar?' I pointed out patiently.

She gawked at me, her mouth open – never a good look, unless your tongue's checking out her tonsils. 'Because . . .'

'Go on,' I encouraged.

'Umm . . . the sunshine's too harsh? Skin cancer?' She shrugged and laughed, the idiot. 'But you know what they say – slip, slap, slop!' She frowned. 'Or is it flip, flap, flop?'

'For frig's sake, Maria! – I'm not TALKING about preventing melanoma!'

'Who's she? Prevent her from doing what?'

'Skin cancer, you clown!' I grabbed her wrists. 'I'm talking about YOU and ME!'

'Oh.' She looked resigned. 'Them again.'

'God!' I let go of her with one hand and hit it hard against the bike-shed wall. 'You act as though I'm talking about Famine and Pestilence or something –'

'Well, YOU'RE certainly not famine – not with THOSE tits!' She chucked me under the chin; I HATE that. It's the gesture most designed and guaranteed to make you feel fat, EVER. 'My little Pesty!'

'Maria –' I took both her hands in mine again and held them against my – well, GROIN, I suppose; there's no nice word for it. She looked around guiltily, though no one but us ever bothered to go behind the boring old bike sheds for a fag any more – they were all off smoking crack behind the science annexe. I spoke to her low and urgent. 'Maria, if I DID go to live in the Bahamas, how do you think we'd ever get to keep this – US – going?'

'Well, there's always email . . .'

'Email!' I held her hands against my – well, breasts I suppose! I know, it's getting a bit pervy, innit? But I could have cried when the look on her face suggested that I'd plunged them into a steaming vat of dog-mess. Kim-like, I soldiered on. 'Maria . . . how can email take the place of THIS . . . of touching, of flesh . . .'

She considered briefly. 'Well, not right NOW maybe – but in a few years' time we'll all have cyber-sex dungeons in our houses, like in *The Lawnmower Man*!'

I let go of her hands and jumped up – I'd had enough, with a cherry on top – but she was quicker than me and grabbed me, pushing me back against the bike-shed wall. 'What? What have I done wrong now?'

'Wanting me to go – ' I hung my head, my hair hanging over my face.

She pushed it back gently and then, not so gently, kept my head held back against the wall. 'Oh, I'm SUCH a BITCH, innit! Because I want you to leave Skid-Row-on-Sea, and a houseful of smelly men, boys, whatever, and go

158

to a beautiful place where the sun always shines and your rich mum's waiting for you. Ooh, wicked, wicked Sugar!'

I yelped – because each of the last three words was accompanied by a banging of my head against the wall; a moderate banging, but a banging nevertheless.

She let go of me then, and hands on her hips (this, I was rapidly deciding, was her natural position of repose) gave me a piece of her mind. Look, don't knock it, she only had a piece the size of a teabag to start with!

'What is it with you, Kim? Why am I some sort of bitch-cow from hell, just because I can see more than myself – and more than "Me-an'-you"? Well, you may think "Me-an'-you" is the be-all and end-all of life, but from where I'm standing it's more like a DEAD end. What's your dream, Kim? – that we just get deeper and deeper into this, and then in a couple of years' time you don't even go away to college? Then we both get crap jobs and we never see each other anyway, and what was it all for? For "Me-an'-you"! Big fat frigging deal!'

I couldn't believe how she was justifying her own slaggy shallowness by pretending to, like, care about my FUTURE or something fancy like that! I shook myself, smoothed down my hair and made to leave; I had a hot date with The Rock, remember, discipline and humiliation a speciality. I turned to look at her; she was STILL glaring at me like I was in the wrong!

'Look, I've got to go and get shouted at. All I want to say is – Sugar, if you don't feel anything for me, why not just say so? Just say it, and all this boring . . . THING that's such a drag for you will be over. Face it, I'm never going to be a stalker – I'm too short for one thing, I'd look silly. Just stop pretending you CARE, that's all I'm asking, when you obviously feel nothing –'

She took the hands off her hips and the glare off her face then, and it was weird – I could tell she was trying to de-Sugar herself in some way, become the sort of boring, mature, solid citizen who isn't really a teenager in anything but years. (Me, as I used to be?) You could almost see her placing her limbs and features in the way she thought normal people looked! – no attitude or aggression or edge. I should have been pleased, I know, to see the hard, shiny shell come off, however briefly – at last, the Real You! – but to be frank it gave me the creeps. Seeing her try to appear harmless made me feel incredibly frightened, as though what she was about to say would be the worst thing I could imagine, and that she was trying to seem civilized in order to make it hurt less.

I knew she was about to dump me.

'Kim.' She folded her hands in front of her. 'Just because I can't feel everything, it doesn't mean I can't feel anything. I'm sorry if what I feel isn't enough for you. But maybe, for me, it's as much in its own way – like dog years and people years. Maybe it's the same, I don't know, proportion, fraction, of my feelings for you as yours are for me. But the size of our feelings were different to start with. You know what I'm saying?'

I nodded suspiciously. Was she dumping me, or had she been smoking dope?

'But, Kim, sometimes I feel that even if what I felt for you was the size of, I don't know, the Grand Canyon –'

'Which is EMPTY!' I pounced pointlessly.

'All right then, THE SIZE OF THE SEA. But even if what I felt was THAT MUCH, I still get the feeling it wouldn't be ENOUGH for you. And that makes me feel like, why bother?'

'It IS enough –' I couldn't believe the deed wasn't done, that I still had a chance to put my case. 'The past few months, it's made me more happy, less scared of stuff, than I've ever been – it's like my life just began, and it's the most brilliant song, after a load of rubbish intro. My life seemed so small before, and now it's all big, just superimposed over everybody else's, and it's like I'm looking down on them from a tall building, like they're ants, just going about their silly business and none of it matters.'

She nodded. 'See, I think that's probably how you tell a good thing from a bad one, 'specially at our age. A good thing makes your life bigger – a bad one makes it smaller. But sometimes it's different stuff for different people, and sometimes it changes. So this – what we've got – is good now, because before me, let's face it, you had this really sad little life. But if it – us – stopped you from living a brilliant life somewhere else, it'd become a bad thing. If you don't think you'd like it out there with your mum, fair enough, you're not sacrificing anything. But in the future, when it comes to college, you might really truly want something else. And you might not go for it because of us – me. And that would make us a bad thing, and the good stuff we had wouldn't count for nothing.' She came up to me, held me by the shoulders. 'That's all, love. That's all I wanted to say.' Then she took me in her long arms and hugged me tight.

I could barely speak. I was so full of happiness that I thought it might actually come up my throat and out of my mouth like a big shining blob of mercury.

After a bit she pushed me gently away. She tidied my hair, smiling, but she was her old glinting self again. 'Go on, see The Rock. And make sure you show her who's boss. Ain't NOBODY disses my bitch!'

13

Well, the telling off from The Rock wasn't anything to write home about – blah, blah, drugs are a waste of precious young potential, better things to do at your age, high on life itself, you're not just letting yourself down, you're letting me down and you're letting the school down; as the inflatable head of the inflatable school said to the inflatable pupil with the PIN! – boom boom! She DID say that if I was ever caught necking E or otherwise getting out of it on drugs again I'd be excluded for a WAAAY long time and that would totally screw up my exams and – horrors – put me back a year. But, actually, I DO take my exams seriously and I do NOT intend to get caught with anything stronger than cough medicine again, and even then I'll make sure it's the non-drowsy kind.

But the letter that came a few days later was a piece of work indeed. It had a Bahamas stamp on it, but it obviously came from Loonyville. It purported to be written by my 'mother', one Stella Lewis, but was clearly the work of an escaped lunatic, probably about fifteen and definitely educationally subnormal, hell-bent for some reason on making said Mother look like she was certifiably brain-dead. Written on 'Love Is . . .' notepaper, the missive was smeared in suntan oil and barely legible, but from what I could make out the drift was that my alleged parent misses me 'even more than Corrie – by the way can you start taping the omnibus this week and bring as many as poss with you when you come?' and had 'seen the most gorgeous sarong in Miss Mae's Fine Things that I've bought and hung up in your bedroom; well it's the junk room at the mo, but we'll sort it out the minute you say you're coming. It's a lovely pink, really unusual, and won't make you look a bit washed out and sort of dish-watery blonde the way most pinks do, darling. You see, I remembered!'

Dad had kept it from Matthew that Stella had been back in town, and I thought it was best we kept it that way. I was already up and about when the letter came and I pocketed it quick, reading it on the bus, but keeping it from Sugar lest she offer to pack my case and take me to the airport. Besides, she had other things on her mind.

'Parents' Evening tonight then, Kizzy!' She bounced excitedly on the wall. 'Make sure you get your dad looking half-tasty, for my mum!' She leered horrendously. 'Try and get him to wear Simon!'

Honestly, this isn't as perverted as it sounds; 'Simon' is simply what she calls this shirt she saw Dad wearing once, that she says Simon from Blue has too. Personally, I'd always thought it was one of his even-more-regrettable-than-usual fashion faux pas; white linen-mix, double-breasted and high-necked, it made him look like one of those saddos who go about passing themselves off as doctors and then get found out when they put someone's heart on the wrong side. See, the trouble is that Dad was in his twenties in the eighties and got carried away with that New Romantics crap, and he doesn't realize, as sadults never do, that what may well have looked flamboyant and dramatic – be it a double-breasted linen-mix shirt, a military jacket with brass buttons or tartan trews – on a lean young body under a firm young jawline and glossy young hair looks instead desperate and amateur-dramatic – like you set out for a fancy-dress party but lost your nerve halfway and abandoned a few key accessories on the bus – on a saggy, baggy body under advancing jowls and receding hairline.

I shrugged, but she was off on one. Honestly, I had no objection to Maria having lustful thoughts, but couldn't she have directed them towards the most recent generation of the Sweet and Lewis families – young and firm and, um, HOT as we were – rather than drool over the prospect of our ancestors getting their gammy legs over each other? I had enough to deal with having a mother who was a cross between Lolita and Mrs Robinson, a really inferiority-complex-engendering blend of dollyness and decadence; I don't think I was ready for a father who couldn't decide between boy-band wannabe and dirty doctor.

'Just think, we'd be SISTERS . . .' she sniggered.

'Sugar! STOP it! You know that gives me the creeps.'

'Why? 'S'no pervier than what we're doing already –'

'Pervy! You and me! What's pervy about it?'

'Ewww . . . what isn't!' She jumped off the wall as the final bell went and set off, stalking across the playground, me almost running on my little baby legs to keep up. 'I meant that in a GOOD way,' she reassured me over her shoulder.

'Ma-RIA!' I chased after her, intent on getting an

answer before we were swallowed up by the straitjacket of the school day. But what do you know, I couldn't keep up with her.

But then, I never could.

Thankfully, Dad didn't wear 'Simon' – just what a blessing this was I didn't fully grasp until we drew close to the gates of Preston High. (Wouldn't you know, the Parents' Night was being held at the stuck-up dive, in theory so that the sadults could see the full glory of yob–snob cooperation, but in reality so they wouldn't have to dwell on what an über-dump they'd sent their little darlings to.) There, coming towards us, was a smirking Maria and a shivering Suzy in what looked like a porn star's idea of a make-do nurse's uniform – black heels, black tights, a blue-and-white striped skirt (horizontal) and a tight white top, with a back-to-front white baseball cap perched incongruously on her head.

'Kizza! KIZZY!' yelled Sugar, holding up poor Suzy's hand and waving it triumphantly. They began to run towards us – looking sort of like a beautiful, heartless panther dragging along a mild-mannered scarecrow dressed for a swingers' session, if you squinted. Maria skidded to a standstill right in front of us, beaming broadly at both of us but mostly at Dad, her mother gripped firmly but fairly around the wrist.

'Hello, Mr Lewis! You don't half look nice tonight! Doesn't he – MUM?' You've never heard a beautiful teenage girl nudge-nudge, wink-wink so much like an ugly old man, I promise you.

To give Suzy credit, she wasn't stupid – just good-natured, which I'm afraid in this nasty world often seems like one and the same to those of a more savage mind. She winced and shrugged as she smiled at us, and made us well aware that we were all in this together – i.e. humouring Ninny the Natural, who was really quite normal a lot of the time so long as she remembered to shave the soles of her feet when the moon was full.

'Shame you didn't wear Simon though, Nate,' my demented love was now musing horrifically. I grabbed her by the arm and dragged her on through the gates of Preston High, and she giggled, put her arm around my waist and rested her head on my shoulder. Behind us I could feel Dad and Suzy's bafflement about the status of the absent Simon melt away into innocent approval of our girlish friendship.

'Look great together, don't they?' whispered my match-making pal, leering back over her shoulder at the totally mismatched, awkward, silent pair. 'Suzy Lewis! Jesus Lewis, She-Ra Lewis, Evil-Lyn Lewis –'

'STELLA Lewis,' I put in pointedly.

'Not for long though I bet, innit! She'll be divorcing your old bloke and marrying the rich boyfriend before everything finally goes south.' Seeing my face she giggled and squeezed me tight. 'Wonder if they'll make us share a bedroom!'

I wriggled away from her; unusual, I know, but this sort of parental pimping made me feel distinctly unsexy. I knew LOGICALLY that there wasn't any such thing as a 'white-trash' mentality, but Maria's oft-repeated desire to make me her stepsister–sex-partner brought to mind unfortunate images of Southern-accented, trailer-dwelling participants in American television talk shows, where Bob was not just your uncle but probably your grandad and nephew too – and, after a suitable surgical adjustment, your Aunt Roberta.

'It's just what JJ needs, a man about the house,' the Machiavellian minx nodded wisely. 'Teach him about man-stuff – fishing, driving, what to do if your foreskin's too tight –'

'PLEASE!' I pulled away and marched on ahead, barging in through the school's main entrance; to be frank, and maybe I was being snobbish, I couldn't think of anything worse than having the Sweet ménage – menagerie! – descend on our spacious, well-ordered house in sedate Preston Park. As I thought this, I suddenly realized that I'd stopped thinking of my home as a hollow shell, somewhere that was wasting away in the shadow of Stella's absence; I thought of it as not such a bad place after all, and actually somewhere, on balance, I wanted to keep it as it was. When I thought of the Sweets bringing ALL THAT STUFF to it, I felt offended and protective of the frail, abandoned thing that Dad, Matthew and I had somehow nursed back to some sort of life. Sure, it wasn't the sort of 'family home' you saw on the gravy commercials – but then, it never had been. It may have struck some people as 'broken' – but didn't broken things often end up stronger on the joins?

I heard Maria chuckling demonically as she stalked after me, and Dad calling to me to wait up, and scooted round the corner right slap bang into the past. My nose hit a beautifully cut blazer, my shoulders were steadied by strong, dark hands, and I was enveloped in the familiar, expensive smell of lime-and-leather cologne.

Zoe's father laughed. 'Hello, little stranger. Long time no see.' I looked past him and saw Zoe glaring, Mrs Clements gazing distractedly around her – and, would you credit it, Polly Hobart holding possessively on to Mr Clements's arm, looking like the cat who got the canary. Until he shook her off to embrace me, that is.

'Where you been, girl? House ain't the same without you goin' round testing all the smoke alarms!'

OK, I know I'm boring. I only did this twice, I swear. I smiled at him. 'Hello, Mr Clements, oh, you know, I've just been –'

'Nate!' Saint Senior boomed, pulling me with him as he strode up to Dad, Suzy and Sugar. Then he was doing that hail-fellow-well-met thing that you had to be black and buff not to look like an absolute antique tosspot doing, throwing one arm across Dad's shoulder and pumping his hand up and down at the same time.

I saw Dad wince; David Clements had a mighty grip, honed originally on the mean streets of London, but more recently and thoroughly on the golf course, where he was a legend in his own leisure-time. A totally self-made, scarily self-assured man, he delighted in taking white bourgeois clichés and bending them to his whim, for his own amusement, in a way he considered unique to himself. Mrs C was one of those guilty-white-girl-World-Music types, and they'd somehow contrived to meet at the Notting Hill Carnival; no doubt her husband's deliberate and elaborate bourgeoisification explained her constant look of befuddlement. He was tricky, but all in all he was pretty sorted for a sadult.

He dipped his head brusquely but courteously in the direction of Suzy and Maria, and then of me.

'Excusez-moi, ladies.'

'Ladies? Where?' Zoe was smirking. I swear she was a good three inches bigger than she'd been last term, almost as tall as her dad, and even more sculpted than she had been, and sort of golden. 'Oh. Hi, Kim. Maria. And –' She peered curiously at Suzy, taking in every excruciating element of her nearly-nurse's outfit.

'Hello, love. I'm Maria's mum,' smiled Suzy affably. It was so weird about Mrs Sweet – she'd spent her life on the roughest, toughest estate in Brighton, and she had absolutely no idea about the profound evil that lurked within the human psyche. Especially the teenage variety.

'Of COURSE you are,' Saint oozed. 'I SO see the resemblance. And you came straight from work! – at the A & E – ' she elaborated, as if we hadn't all got it.

Then a brilliant thing happened. I'd always realized that Mr Clements was off-the-graph proud of Zoe, but he was proud of her in a different way to any other parent I'd seen. Far from making him indulge her, as is usual with favoured kids, his pride instead made him treat her like an almost-equal, like a challenging wannabe-alpha-beast who had to be cut down to size whenever she tried to throw her weight around in front of him – and, boy, did she need it.

But I'd never seen it done QUITE this excellently; the diss hadn't even been full-stopped before his arm shot out and curled gently around his daughter's head, his big hand covering her mouth. Her eyes widened in shock and horror and the Sweet-Lewises all laughed – Maria like a hyperactive coyote.

'David –' Mrs Clements stepped out of her husband's hinterland at last, every syllable sounding like a sigh. 'Let go of Zoe now –'

He whipped his hand away from Zoe's gob and laid it on my shoulder. 'Come and walk with me, Li'l Kim.' With this, Polly leaped forward – like one of those dreadlocked dogs, though nowhere near as cute or independent-minded – ready to take up her place at Mr Clements's right hand once more, but he smiled ruefully. 'Ain't seen my girl Kim in an age, Poll-Doll. Be back real soon.' She fell back, joining Zoe in shooting me daggers, and I wondered where HER parents were. Obviously they were whiter than white, and she'd misled them as to the date of Parents' Night rather than be identified as albino-spawn.

The chance to escape Maria's perverted family-planning project AND piss off Po-Ho was more than I could resist – and I set off, scurrying at his side, keeping up with his stride.

'Science Fair!' he boomed, pointing. 'That'll do us, won't it, Kim?' He turned to the trailing tribes of Sweets, Clementses, Lewises and Hobarts behind us. 'My down-girl

Kim and I are off to check out this Science Fair, perchance to share some quality time. We'll see you back here in twenty minutes or so.'

I was aware of various glaring (Zoe, Polly), puzzling (Mrs C, Mrs S and Mr L) and smirking (Sugar, with me gone, all the better to throw our elders together), but Mr C was an alpha male and his word was law and they let us move away without protest. We took a left, then a right and came face to face with the shiny smorgasbord of the Science Fair, all blow-ups of fractals and cell modules and what have you. Science has never been my strong suit, which is odd because AS YOU KNOW BY NOW I'm quite boring. I guess that to like science you've got to be gung-ho about your own dreariness, and typically I'm even apologetic about that.

Mr Clements pointed at a big drawing of DNA and shook his head, sort of sorrowful but stern, sort of Old-Testamenty-when-will-they-ever-learn. 'That thing –'

'DNA?'

'Yeah. Whatever. That meant to be the mystery of life solved. No?'

'I think so. Sort of.'

'WRONG!' He said it loud, but it wasn't angry or embarrassing like you'd think. People looked, but only in an interested way, like they wanted to come closer and get in on the thing. 'Li'l Kim, do you know when the mystery of life will be solved?'

'Um –' You never knew whether Mr Clements wanted you to answer or just be an audience.

'The MYSTERY of LIFE will be SOLVED, baby girl,' he boomed, and this WAS a bit embarrassing now, 'when SCIENTISTS can EXPLAIN the unique APPEAL of the SMELL of a BABY'S HEAD. And the SORROW and the WHY of how the baby loses that smell.'

DNA thus cut down to size, we wandered on, stopping in front of an exhibition labouring under the title THE FAMILY OF MAN: ONE RACE – THE HUMAN RACE! It was as yucky as it sounds, and the worst thing was this horrible computer-generated poster of a monkey-thing with these – UDDERS, you'd have to call them, right down to its stomach, gazing out at us soulfully. Apparently it was M'REI – MOTHER OF MAN.

Mr Clements whistled low and shook his head. 'Man, my mother looked like that, I'd have died of fright before they cut the cord.'

I gurgled with politically incorrect glee and Mr Clements did the hair-rumpling thing again. He gestured to a couple of uncomfy-looking chairs and we went and sat down on them, pretending to be absorbed in the tragic display.

'So, you and Miss Thing – what happened?' Mr Clements said non-committally, gazing at a giant plastic split-sectioned womb as if the answer might slide down one of the Fallopian tubes at any moment.

I shrugged. 'Oh, you know . . . girl stuff. Teenage stuff. Nothing important.'

'If girl stuff and teenage stuff ain't important to a teenage girl, I'd like to know what is!' he laughed. Then he looked serious. 'You don't haveta tell me, Kim – I love my daughter, but in my book that means I'm not scared of knowing her either. Lots of people like to use love as a blindfold, but that's not my thing – that's for weak people. No, the way I look at it, Zoe's been coming the royal bitch on a regular basis. And even though you're such a good girl and a good friend, one day you'd just had enough. Am I right?'

I hesitated, went to lie as a sort of reflex, then stopped, realizing I was safe to tell the truth with Mr Clements, that he was that rare creature, AN ADULT WHO DIDN'T HAVE TO BE PROTECTED. So I burst out laughing and nodded. 'That's about it. And she was cross that I changed schools – said I was abandoning her –'

I looked at Mr Clements then and knew that I'd been wrong, and that you could never really tell the truth to Them, no matter how cool they seemed. His face was all hard and closed in on itself and it was like he was talking to himself too when he said, 'And with your mother runnin' out and all . . . and she still said that to you . . .' He laughed softly and it was like some sort of despair.

I put my hand on one of his. 'It's not her fault –'

He snapped out of it and smiled kindly at me. 'It's her fault and my fault too – I don't know if that halves the blame or doubles it. Anyway, what's done is done. I guessed as much. I don't blame you for bailing out – I just feel sorry for me and Zoe's mum. That Polly! – talk about annoying.'

I smiled politely. He didn't like Po-Ho and that was just

174

fine by me. He smiled back and put his hand out to me and we walked back the way we'd come.

They were kicking their heels in an awkward clump of clusters; Zoe and Polly muttering darkly, Maria smirking as Dad and Suzy made awkward conversation. Everyone bar Sugar looked relieved when Mr Clements walked right in and took control.

'Nate, we'd better get in there and see those teachers. Mrs – Sweet? How appropriate! Well, lets us big folk go and do the nasty, shall we? You kids – you don't need to come. I know teachers these days, and they're soft – they won't wanna hurt your baby feelings in case you grow up to be an axe murderer that sues them for inflicting low self-esteem. Whyn't you go outside and, I don't know, do whatever you girls do. Pull each other's hair and stuff.' He winked at me and led the other docile adults away.

I knew his game; he was trying to make me go in and fight for Zoe. That was why he'd dissed poor Po-Ho. He may have been smart for a sadult, but how little idea he had of how the power thing worked down here in GirlWorld! She was a Top Girl, and I was a B Girl; we didn't make stuff happen. Our only weapon was a negative one – walking away when we'd finally had enough of being a sticky combination of emotional punchbag, groupie and bag-carrier. And I'd played that card already.

'Your dad's a bit of the Big I-Am, ain't he?' Maria observed to Zoe. 'See where you get it from. Quite fit though, for a –' She broke off and grabbed my arm. 'Come on, let's chill in the crazy playground.'

We were no sooner out the door than Zoe and Po-Ho piled out too, Zoe blazing and Po bristling. Zoe went straight up to Sugar and shoved her against a wall. I was amused, though slightly disturbed, to see Sugar smile slinkily and go, 'Ooh . . . you're hard, ain't you?'

'What were you going to say?' Zoe demanded. 'Back there? That you didn't finish?'

'Oh.' Sugar furrowed her brow theatrically. 'I don't remember. It's hard to think when you're getting me all worked up with your big tough ways.' Saint released her; Maria brushed herself down fastidiously. 'Shame. I was enjoying that. But no doubt it won't be the last time you lose that nasty temper of yours.'

'What were you going to say?' Zoe demanded. 'About my dad?'

'What, that he's as bossy as you are?'

'NO! That he was – quite fit – for a –?'

'For a –?' Maria smiled innocently. 'Oh yeah. I was going to say, for an old bloke.'

'No you weren't! You were going to say "for a black"!'

'Was I?' Maria seemed genuinely perplexed.

'Seen, y'all,' Po-Ho muttered smugly. It must have been the fulfilment of a major fantasy for her, being involved in a genuine racial conflict. All we needed was a few Uzis and she'd have died of ecstasy.

'I wasn't, you know.' Maria shook her head seriously, took my arm and led me on to the playing fields.

'You WERE!' Zoe yelled, following us.

'Well thank you, Gypsy Queen, for reading my mind

so deeply that you even know stuff about me that I don't have a clue about!' Sugar sniggered. 'You want to get yourself a booth on the pier and charge for it.' She turned and faced her. 'Or you could come and have a smoke with us. Help you calm down a bit.'

We walked on, aware of them murmuring as they followed. Finally we stopped and sat on the grass. Maria took out a spliff and lit up.

Zoe glared down at us. I was amused to see that Po-Ho was puzzled as to what attitude she should adopt: disapproving, like her indignant idol, or well pleased because, well, it WAS a spliff after all. She finally settled her face into a frown, albeit a greedy one, when Zoe spoke as Sugar handed the joint to me.

'I can't believe you're doing that. On school premises. After all that in the papers about you collapsing on E! I bet you any money you've been warned by your head that you'll be chucked out if you're caught doing drugs again.'

Maria sniggered.

'Fool,' said Zoe contemptuously. 'I wouldn't expect you to understand. Let's face it, you don't even have a future to wreck. There'll always be jobs going at Burger King.'

That snob thing she did! – I SO hated it. She hadn't changed a bit. That made my mind up; I took a long draw on the smoking gun I held in my right hand. Then, just to be extra naughty, I offered it to Polly. 'It's real good stuff,' I twinkled.

'You dare!' Zoe exploded. She turned on her heel and

marched away. Polly stood there poleaxed; I swear her lower lip wobbled.

'C'mon – get down with the "hood",' drawled Maria. 'Whatchoo waiting for?'

'POLLY!' came the incensed yell, and with that Po-Ho took off in the direction of her master's voice.

Maria took the joint from me and sucked it luxuriously. She shook her head wonderingly. 'Look at that. Like a little dog. Honestly! – that's not a friendship!'

The dope had made me woozy; I leaned over and tried to kiss her. She brushed me off almost without thinking about it. 'Look at us – that's a friendship. Equal. Considerate. What are you laughing at? Kim? Kim!'

I shook my head helplessly.

'You're weird, you are.' She jumped to her feet and hauled me up. 'Come on, let's go and see whether we're going to be doing incest soon!'

14

They say forewarned is forearmed, but I think that to be forewarned would be to be frozen by sorrow and dismay. Imagine you're dying, fading away with some terrible disease, and you've been given the gift of knowing that that was the LAST time you're going to walk outside and feel the sun on your face, the LAST time you're going to look at the face of someone you love before you go blind. It would break your heart even more than it was broken already.

I've always been told I was clever and felt sorry for ignorant people, but as I get older I really believe more and more that ignorance is bliss. With the benefit of hindsight, if that's not a contradiction. But hell, why SHOULDN'T it be a contradiction? Everything else is. Love even – love ESPECIALLY. For all I can tell, for a lot of people, loving someone, and having them love you, means you can treat them any way you like. Even though it's MEANT to mean you treat them the best you possibly can.

Look at Stella and Maria with me – now that's two different types of love, the two main types I would say. I certainly loved them and they said they loved me back. But I just get the feeling that if I HADN'T loved them, they'd have been a lot nicer to me.

I'll get back to Stella – let her wait a while, like I did for her. Maria was the main event, albeit in an almost totally negative way. As the term progressed, so our relationship did the opposite. Of course, the long school holiday was over, and even at weekends autumn doesn't offer the same opportunities for quality time (and canoodling) as lazy-day fun in the sun does. That was HER excuse anyway.

'But isn't it nice to be all warm inside when it's all stormy outside?' I pleaded selfishly when she declared that she had Seasonal Affective Disorder, and this was putting her off, well, the PHYSICAL side of things.

'Not for me it's not. Stuck in that poxy little house with a sex maniac and two evil dwarfs. And no cable!' She sniffed, ''S'all right for you. See, if your dad and my mum hooked up, no problemo.'

'But then we'd be cramped here!'

'Na, your dad wouldn't want JJ and the trolls around. He'd pay for them to go to boarding school. It'd be just us!' She squeezed my arm. 'We'd be real cosy then!'

And so it would start, and once again a couple of precious hours at my briefly otherwise empty house would be wasted on the jerry-building of castles in the sky in which Maria, myself, Suzy and Dad would live happily ever after, complete with 199 cable TV channels and no skanky siblings. When I would finally convince her that Dad could barely afford to send a dog to a kennel for a long weekend, let alone three kids to boarding school for years on end, she would change tack and ask why we couldn't go and live with Stella in the Bahamas. 'I bet I'd want sex all the time there!' she leered unconvincingly.

I'd been dumb enough to tell her that Stella had taken to calling me once a week, every Sunday evening, which is clever psychology when you consider the feelings of school-related boredom and fear that blight even the most carefree of kids at this point. Dad knew all about her suggestion and was doing his wise-old-owl thing, sitting and keeping his counsel – I think he knew that he'd been out of order slagging Stella off like that to the local rag, which is good because it HAD been an amazingly loony thing to do. So now he bit his tongue and looked brave (and a bit bittersweet) and said that I must make my own mind up about what I wanted. Except we mustn't tell Matt until I'd decided, because there was no point in upsetting him for nothing.

Well, he wouldn't be upset, because I wasn't going to leave. I kept telling her so. Of course I couldn't tell her why – that the one person who made my senses sing and my blood rush was in Brighton, and that I had to be with her in order to even BREATHE. Though the sex side wasn't all it could be, while I was still physically with her there was always a chance of sparking it up again. If I was in another country I was lost, and so was she – lost to me forever.

Even as it was, I could feel her slipping away. More and more, I'd call for her on a weekend afternoon and she'd be out; dog-like, I'd jump at the chance of waiting for her when Suzy, the twins or even JJ casually suggested it. I marvelled at how throwaway they were about the chance of seeing her, the mundane miracle of her return, the thrill of hearing her key in the door, of feeling it turn in my heart. How could Suzy ever imagine that I must have lots of better things to do, a pretty girl like me, than wait for Ave to come home? What better thing could there be than to be with her?

Actually, waiting for her was starting to be better than being with her; often, she was more THERE when I was waiting for her than she was when she actually arrived. When I was waiting, my imaginary, anticipated Maria told me all the things I longed to hear, touched me everywhere I wanted to be touched, slowly and in strict sequence – like an easy, sleazy treasure hunt, looking and finding and, well, TREASURING what she found there, I suppose. OK! I know it's tragic. But at least it's mine. And here at least I could rule unridiculed over my tragic kingdom – whereas in the various regions of the real world I'd visited so far, I seemed always to end up as a pawn, a raw prawn, a punch-line to a joke that wasn't even funny. A bad pun, maybe.

I remembered this day in particular because it was the day before The Play – which means that it was The Last Time, like I was banging on about earlier. I'd gone round to Sugar's house after tea, ostensibly to do revision, but hope-fully – because Suzy was working a late shift and the kids were all sleeping-over elsewhere – to do the deed. To ease the way towards my evil ends, I had two half-bottles of Smirnoff smouldering coldly in my schoolbag. As I'd stowed them I'd had a bit of a hang-on-a-minute moment, as the unwelcome thought hit me that it was usually ugly young boys or dirty old men who needed to use hard liquor to help them have their wicked way – not teenage hotties like my sweet self. But then I remembered the taste of her skin, and I gave my better judgement its marching orders.

There was simply no contest; common sense – or rare magic?

Suzy answered the door dressed in her uniform, and seemed mildly surprised to see me. 'She's not back yet, love – went right back out after her tea. I'm off now, but you're welcome to come in and watch the telly. She'll remember soon, I s'pect.' She laughed and called over her shoulder as she closed the front door, 'Why don't you have a test of all them lovely smoke alarms you put up for us?'

I sat down gloomily on the sofa and flicked through the channels. Another crack about smoke alarms! I swear, I only did it once at each house, the Sweets' and the Clements'. Yet it seemed to be my most distinguishing feature. Other teenagers became urban legends for, I don't know, dancing really well or doing something new and dangerous on a skateboard; I was obviously going to be a playground legend due to my high standards of safety in the home. When kids approvingly called each other 'Safe', I really don't think this is what they had in mind.

I turned the TV off, took an eye-watering hit of neat vodka and started to wander restlessly round the room. They had one of those unit things, with bits of divided shelf for different stuff. Videos and CDs fought for space in their sections, but a lone book stood proudly in its solitary splendour: *Secrets of the Sex-o-Scope* by Belladonna Bellini. I took it down and thumbed through it mournfully, looking up Sugar's star sign, Gemini. Apparently her Top-Ten Turn-Offs were:

Swearing
Cheap or tarty clothes
Lateness
People who flick their hair
Annoying laughs
Lack of ambition
Flirts
Chewing gum
Loudmouths
People who can't handle their drink

I laughed hollowly; if Sugar really did dislike the things on this list, then she'd have a chronic case of self-loathing, which somehow I didn't think was the case. And thank goodness the last vice on the list was one of her greatest –

The door slammed and I put the book back guiltily. She ambled in, wearing jeans tight enough to show her age, right down to the month, and a crop-top brief enough to deny it; hand on the Bible and I-swear-Your-Honour-I-thought-she-was-at-least-seventeen-and-three-quarters. At first I thought she hadn't noticed me; she went straight to the sofa and picked up the remote. She zapped the TV into life, and I felt as though she held another, invisible controller in her hand as well, one with which she could bring me to life, pause me and shut me down, all at her whim.

'Oh. YOU'RE here.' Her voice was neither pleased nor disapproving.

'We said so – at lunchtime – don't you remember?'

'Na. Musta been thinking of something else.'

'Well, you WERE picking a scab off your knee at the time –' I stopped myself; pathetically, I was trying to put this nasty personal habit forward as some sort of legitimate excuse for her mistreatment of me!

'Oh, right.' She changed channels.

'So where were you?'

'Oh. Around –'

'Your mum said you went straight back out –'

'Did she? That's nice.'

'So who were you –'

She jumped to her feet and glared at me. 'So! When did it happen?'

'When did what happen?'

'The new law. My sentence. Whatever. THE THING THAT SAYS I'M UNDER EFFING HOUSE ARREST, THAT'S WHAT!'

'Sorry,' I muttered.

'Oh, don't be sorry! You don't make the laws after all. You're just doing your job. Which is, apparently, BEING MY JAILER.'

There wasn't any answer to that really; 'No I'm not!' sounded simple, like I didn't get the sarcasm. So I sat down uneasily on the Dralon armchair across from the sofa and waited for her to stop seeing me as one of that vast, shadowy army, the one which never slept and had only one aim in mind. TO STOP SUGAR HAVING FUN!

After about ten minutes she said, 'I could murder a drink. But there ain't none in the cabinet. I looked. Just that retsina next door brought back. I'll heave if I touch that.'

I smirked as I played my ace. 'I've got vodka . . .'

She sat up straight and smiled straight at me. Dum-dum bullets straight to my dumb, dumb heart. 'How much?'

'Two half-bottles.' I flourished them, one in each hand. 'Give us one!'

I threw one to her and she caught it one-handed; it was a very romantic moment, all dashing and chivalrous and courtly love and that – like I'd come to her rescue and spread out my cloak for her to walk on. She unscrewed the cap and drank greedily; 'That's more like it!'

She eyed me; since I met Sugar, I had come to believe that 'eyeing' someone is quite different to looking at them. If you're 'eyeing', it's like your eye is an actual instrument, a pointed stick or something, and you're using it to sort of poke at a person with. She was definitely doing that now. 'Well, you. What have you got to say for yourself?'

'What d'you mean?' I said nervously. She didn't adopt this tone of voice often, but I found it hard to deal with when she did. It was an old-fashioned, nineteen-eighties-soap-opera-vamp sort of voice; a gay divorcee in skyscraper shoulder pads like I'd seen on UK Gold 'toying' with her 'prey'. I didn't like being toyed with, I'd discovered.

'Don't come the innocent with me.' She took another swig, wiped her mouth with the back of her hand and wagged a finger at me. 'Come round here . . . everybody out . . . ply me with drink . . .' She crossed the room and sat on my lap, leering ludicrously down at me. It was so much the result I'd wanted, yet at the same time totally wrong;

then it struck me that my vodka wasn't perhaps the first alcoholic beverage to pass those sugar-pink lips that day.

'You've been drinking.' It was out before I could think better of it. My tone wasn't even censorious, but it was a dumb thing to say, considering that I was only here under sufferance and also that, sadly, it was only alcohol which had softened and sexed-up her 'feelings', if that isn't a horrible perversion of the word, towards me.

She drew back and looked at me, her leer become a sneer. 'Ooh. And are you complaining about that – thish – state of affairs?' She gestured wildly with her half-bottle of Smirnoff, spilling some.

'No.' I cast my eyes down, but that meant I was looking at her groin, so I looked up again. Now I was staring straight at her breasts! I turned and looked away in what I hoped was a contemplative, reflective, even regretful fashion.

'LOOK AT ME WHEN I'M TALKING TO YOU!' She grabbed my chin and pulled my face roughly right up to hers. 'No, I bet you're not. But it's a nice change that, that you're not complaining. WHINING. Nagging at me for sex. Like you usually are.'

Tears came to my eyes, like each one was jostling for first prize, and I pushed her away. Drunken fool, she fell sprawling on her dumb ass, and gaped up at me. 'Domestic violence now, is it!'

I felt very grown up and world-weary all of a sudden. 'It wasn't domestic violence, Sugar – you simply fell on your drunken ass. If you weren't so drunk, you'd know that.' I stood up. 'And if I wasn't so sober, I'd stay and take advantage of you. But frankly, from where I'm standing, and from the state of you, it wouldn't be so much kissing as mouth-to-mouth resuscitation. And I'm not that desperate – though sometimes it feels that way – that I'd want to do it with somebody who's too far gone to know which end is which.' I moved towards the door.

I'd never seen her move so fast, Sugar of the tiny feet and languid amble, as she lashed out and rushed in to block my exit, making my apparently smooth flight suddenly unsafe and bumpy. As I was wrestled to the floor I realized that wherever we were heading, I didn't have a map, a clue or a care. So I might as well bail out and follow the crazy one, for all the good it would do me. And this time, we flew –

I couldn't wipe the smile off my face the next day. I stood there in the Ravendene playground, in the warm autumn rain, waiting for her, sure that everything was OK now. When the last bell went I was still smiling as I trooped in.

She came in late, not looking at me. I tried to catch her eye, but she was listening hard to the delights of the day being laid before us. With the luxury of staying perfectly in sync with her, I tuned in too and was reminded that today was the day we were to be favoured with the inevitable crap, caring Social Issues Play that seems to be inflicted on we innocent schoolkiddies, surely the most irretrievably captive audience this side of prison bars, at least twice a term these days. To add insult to injury, the sad bunch of strolling players doing this rotten thing to us were called

PLAYas@SusSEX – The Rock actually spelt it out, with capital letters and all. To give her credit, she did look a bit sick.

'It'll be about sex then,' I murmured to Maria as we stayed in our seats after assembly, waiting for the torment to begin.

She looked at me strangely. 'You'll enjoy it then.'

What the fuck did that mean? Especially in the light of last night. 'Why? And you won't, you mean? Am I some sort of pervert?'

'No.' She smiled and examined her nails. 'But you are a bit of a drama queen.'

It wasn't so much the things she said as the way she said them – as if she was talking to a stranger, and one she suspected she probably wouldn't want to get to know any better too. I'll tell you something creepy I noticed; she was doing the reverse of 'mirroring' me, that thing that shrinks say people do when they meet a new person they're subconsciously attracted to. She was, I don't know, BLOCKING me; if I crossed my legs towards her, she skittered her feet the other way – if I leaned towards her to speak, she drew back and stared. And when I put my arm on the back of her chair, she jerked forward as if the girl behind her had stuck a gun in her back.

It was – the best word, silly as it sounds – UNFRIENDLY. And it hurt. If a mere friend treated you this way you'd feel weird enough; from a lover – and one who less than twenty-four hours previously had been wrapped naked around you tighter than a sex-mad boa constrictor trying to pass as a tourniquet, at that – it was downright freaky. It struck me then that excellently enjoyable though my first attempt at lesbian sex had turned out in many ways, it sometimes made me wonder if being with a boy would really be all that bad. I mean, one of the main reasons girls my age hold back from sleeping with boys is the fear that they're going to freeze you out and put you down the morning after; just throw ALL THAT SOFTNESS you showed them back in your face, as though it was a dirty old sponge or something. Or a custard pie, with you as the punchline! But Maria acted like this all the time these days. And that's when it struck me how much easier it would be to be with a boy; because girls know how to hurt girls – REALLY hurt them.

The one upside to the tears which blurred my vision was that the sadult now striding on to the stage and staring solemnly out at us would have been even more bloody ugly if I'd seen them in focus. I leaned forward to try and work out exactly what gender they were a disgrace to; short ginger hair, skin so angry with adult acne that you should have got free chilli bread with it, skinny up-and-down body clad in grey velour. But by far the most unattractive aspect of the creature was its total and utter humourlessness, obvious even before it spoke a word; its lack of humour came off it in waves, like negative charisma, so blatant that I felt both embarrassed for and angry at this person at the same time.

'Good morning, young citizens of planet Earth,' it said. It was a woman, with a theatrical, cultured, totally clueless voice.

We all sort of mass-mumbled in response, already

embarrassed for her and the rest of the PLAYas. Teenagers are meant to be self-centred and insensitive, but one emotion we DO often feel on behalf of sadults, strangers and (equally strange) loved ones alike, is embarrassment, not for us but for them, and often in advance of the actual tragic act; we're psychic like that, we know EXACTLY when and how they're going to make total twats of themselves. Often we get so embarrassed for them that it makes us angry, and we lose it, and we mock them. BUT THEY STARTED IT!

'My name is Liberty. May I introduce my cosmic companions – Harmony, Diversity and Empowerment.'

What were they, with names like that – pop-stars' kids? Hardly; dressed in the same drab garb, they shambled on looking more like Blear, Drear and Fear. The first two were male, and smug, the last one nominally a woman, shaking like a jelly with a hangover; they were all about as attractive as verruca soup. They lined up and stared at us. 'We come in peace from a planet called Joy,' announced Harmony. 'And we have been observing your earthly ways. And much of what we have seen has grieved us greatly.'

Someone near the front passed wind loudly.

'That's from Uranus – grieve over THAT!' someone shouted from the back and we all snickered with sickening predictability. I looked at Maria hopefully – how sad was that, hoping to bond over mindless flatulence? – but the minute she registered my glance she leaned away and whispered to the girl on the other side of her. They burst out laughing.

'Many aspects of life on your Earth –' (Diversity.)

'– which rhymes with Birth, and Mirth –' (Empowerment, shakily.)

'And Smurf! AND scurf!' (A wit to my left.)

'– are beautiful. Truly you are a blue planet.'

'Blue balls!' shouted someone helpfully.

Liberty pressed on; her inborn humourlessness made her the obvious leader of the group, as well as heckler-defier-in-chief. 'But this embarrassment of riches has made you careless with the manifold jewels in your crown. With the sapphires that are the sky and the sea, with the emerald grass, with the deep rich amber of the earth.'

'Wouldn't wanna step in it!' came a considered riposte from somewhere on my right.

Liberty frowned. 'But the greatest disrespect you display is for the best and most blessed, precious gem you possess. And that jewel, that pearl beyond price – is love. One perfect facet of which is physical love –'

Massive whistling and catcalling ensued. And ensued. The beefiest male teacher on the staff took to the stage and made threatening gestures. The words 'weekend detention' somehow made it through and gradually we all thought better of imitating jackals indefinitely.

'Physical love is love in action. Action is energy. And energy is eternal delight. A delight which can bond a man and a woman. And a woman and a woman –'

'WAHAAAAAAAAAY!'

'And a man and a man.'

'GAAAAAAY!'

'Today, as our gift from the planet Joy, we will make a play, for your pleasure –'

'– in dance and rhyme and mime –' (At this they gurned and pranced shockingly.)

'– which tells of why you, the heirs to planet Earth, must respect the priceless jewel called Love. In whatever shape it reveals itself to our bedazzled eyes.'

Well, it got worse. You couldn't argue with the basic premise of course – that people shouldn't be picked on just because they're gay. But this is SCHOOL, excuse me, and you could just as easily do a play about how wrong it is picking on ginger people, people with glasses and people who put their hands up in class for any other reason than to demand toilet-time. We'll GROW OUT OF IT! In the meantime, doing stuff like this for us makes about as much sense as doing it for a bunch of monkeys in the zoo.

As Liberty, Harmony, Diversity and Empowerment trooped mercifully offstage after the longest twenty minutes in the history of the world (I couldn't help noticing that Liberty grabbed Empowerment's arm the minute she thought they were out of view and shook her like a rag doll while hissing viciously in her face – already wise beyond my years, I presumed they were what is ironically known as 'lovers'), I turned to Maria; surely we would bond over this banquet of cutting-edge lameness?

I nudged her matily. 'Tragic, or what?'

My smile crumbled like a deep-cleansing clay face mask left on too long; her face was colder than an igloo in winter.

She pulled back and rubbed her arm where I had touched her, just staring at me.

'Maria . . . ?'

She nodded, looking thoughtful. 'Yeah. Really tragic.' She stood up, smoothing down her skirt. 'Imagine ever being like them women. Growing up to be some sad, ugly dyke. I'd rather be dead.'

15

It was weird after that – like a ghost world. Except I wasn't clear about whether I was the ghost or the world was. Some days I felt real, sometimes not. Sometimes Sugar seemed real – when she flashed me a reflex smile at someone else's idiocy, a smile as bright and fleeting as a rainbow and causing the same illogical hoping of the heart. Then she remembered not to 'encourage' me and the cloud came over her eyes, and my world turned grey again. There's some old sixties song called 'Sunshine of Your Love' Dad used to like; this was the drizzle of her indifference.

As the autumn took hold and the chill set in I could feel myself become less and less resistant to Stella's Sunday phone calls. When in the last week of October I finally agreed to go out there and visit in the Christmas holidays, she was quite touching in her excitement. I was starting to think we could really have a second chance at building a proper mother–daughter relationship. Until she spoilt it by ending the phone call shouting gleefully, 'I WON, I WON!'

I felt I must have been touched with the glow of a new resolve and confidence when Maria actually came up to me in the playground before school the next day. She was smiling nervously, and I met her eyes boldly.

''Lo, Kimmy –'

'Hi,' I said coolly, pretending to be looking for something in my bookbag.

'We haven't been hanging much recently –'

'Hey, don't sweat it. I understand. Why would you want to hang out with me? You might grow up to be an ugly old dyke.' I was smirking as I trotted towards the entrance.

'Kim –' She took my arm and swung me round. 'I'm real sorry about that. And the way I've been behaving since. I was just . . . panicking, I think. I felt I had to back away. Not because it felt bad – because it felt too good.'

I looked at her from under my eyelashes. I was still a sucker, and she was still as smooth and sweet as a strawberries-and-cream Chupa Chup. 'Do you mean that?'

'Course I do.' She moved in close. 'You doing anything Bonfire Night?'

'No.' I held my breath, like a wide-eyed child waiting for the rocket to slip free of the milk bottle and shoot up into the sky.

'Come to Lewes with me? And then, after – let me sleep over at yours?'

Who needed the sunshine, who needed the Bahamas? Come to that, who needed a mother who needed a mother rather than a daughter? I was looking at all I needed, and my eyes couldn't have been more bedazzled if I'd had all the fireworks in the world going off in front of me.

'Yes. Oh, yes, yes, yes!'

'But WHYYY have you changed your mind?' Surprise surprise, Stella sounded like a spoilt brat, and all the way from

Harbour Island I could hear the stamp of what sounded like her high-heeled foot on Dom's pristine wooden floor.

'I just don't fancy it any more. I've changed my mind. Come on, Mum, you can understand that! You change your mind like you change your thongs.'

'Yes, but . . . YOU don't.'

'Well, that's changed too. We must change or perish. Like the dinosaurs,' I said smugly. Love is the drug that makes you smug.

'Remember when I took you to see Jurassic Park 2?' she said sadly, feeling sorry for herself.

'Yeah. You left me there in the Odeon after ten minutes saying you'd be back soon and went out to buy a bikini and got back half an hour after the film had ended. I was crying in the manager's office.'

'It was totally unsuitable for a young child, that film,' she said primly.

'MUM. I was crying because of YOU. The tyrannosaurus didn't scare me a bit. YOU did.' I could hear I was getting irate, and brought it down a notch. 'Mum – Stella – if I came to live with you, who'd look after us?'

'What do you mean?' I could practically HEAR her trying to make the effort to see things from another point of view. She didn't manage it. 'Oh – I see. Well, we've got a fantastic cook – a maid – gardener – pool boy –'

'Stella. What I mean is, WHO'D BE THE ADULT? When all the help goes home?'

'Well, Dom's very mature –'

'He's twenty or something!'

'Age ain't nuthin' but a number,' she said, sounding really stupid.

I had to laugh then. 'But, Stella – you're going backwards! You're sweet sixteen right now, and swept up in some schoolgirl fantasy of love on Bounty-Bar island, but next year, who knows, you could be TEN! And then you won't want to be with Dom, because he'll be too old for you! You'll want to, I don't know, go back to school or university or something and live in a student flat in Seattle. And what will happen to me? I can't stay with Dom, obviously. And you won't have the money, time or, let's face it, inclination to look after a teenage daughter. So what do I do then? Come back to Brighton and tell Dad he's got to pick up the pieces again – MAKE A FAMILY OUT OF SOME BROKEN UP OLD THING AGAIN? No! He doesn't deserve it, and frankly neither do I. Not to mention what it would do to Matthew. Who's very, very young, for God's sake, in case you've forgottten.'

'Age ain't nuthin' but –'

'No, Stella,' I snapped back angrily. 'Age is everything when your whole world falls apart. Fifteen can handle it. Ten is in a fucking wilderness of pain. And nothing you say can ever change that.'

There was a pause. Then, 'You really hate me, don't you, Kim?'

I had to laugh. Even when she tried to see the other guy's point of view she got it totally wrong. She had to be the centre of attention, even if it was being hated. 'Stella, I don't hate you a bit. I just think you're sort of – sad.'

'What?' I could hear the amazement in her voice. 'But . . . when kids talk about SADULTS – well –' and here the old bumptiousness was coming back already – 'I'm not a BIT like one of those people.'

I laughed, but not nastily – it really was affectionate. I couldn't stop feeling sorry for the silly cow. 'Oh, Stella, you are SO a sadult. Just a different kind. The problem is that no one ever really TOUCHED you – not me, not Matt, not Dad. And so you never really grew up.'

There was a silence. And then some. And then just when the silence got so long that I thought something might FINALLY be sinking in, into the stony, selfish ground of Stella's emotional allotment, the wail burst out; 'But, Kimmy, it's BORING out here!'

I couldn't believe it – and then I laughed in sheer shock, surprised that I was surprised. In her own way, Stella was TOTALLY dependable. You could set your moral clock by her pure self-centredness. 'Say that again, Stella.'

'It's BORING out here, Kimmy! Dom's doing his computer-geek stuff all day – I don't know anyone and they've all been here ages, really stuffy about newcomers . . . there's nothing to do but swim and sun and eat and drink –' She began to whimper then. 'What am I going to DO with my life, Kimmy? You're the most sensible person I know. Just tell me.'

I could do that easily. 'Be brave, Mum. Like I have, and Matt and Dad have, all this time. Just be brave. I know you can do it.'

There was snivelling, then silence. Then – 'Kim?'

'Yes, Mum.' I felt almost tender towards her.

'Could you put Matthew on, please?' I heard the businesslike click of a cigarette lighter, to match her new brisk voice. 'Cos if that's your final word on coming to live with me, I might as well try him.'

I sounded magnificently dignified and controlled, even if I do say it myself, as I finally told the monstrous bitch where to get off. 'No, Stella, I will not put Matthew on. And if you ever attempt to contact him, or in any way mess with his life more than you have already, I will personally tell him that you have sex with dogs.'

Then I hung up.

I was unstoppable.

Love had made me lethal.

We stood close together on the platform, hugging each other to keep the cold out. Jack Frost didn't stand a chance; the combination of love and vodka, all the sweeter for being shared from the half-bottle, kept his prying fingers at bay despite my tiny suede skirt (with boots!) and Maria's low-cut crop top and combats. She grinned at me as the train that would take us to Lewes pulled up at the terminus.

'Gonna be a good night, innit?'

I nodded, too loved up to speak.

'And your dad thinks – knows – I'm gonna stay at yours?'

I made the effort. 'Absolutely.'

'Just in case my mum rings him up, checking. She's been on my case recently. I only stayed out all night the once –'

She stopped then; I followed suit and stopped myself from asking for details. What I didn't know COULD hurt me, but not as much. The train doors opened and we scrambled forward, pushed onwards by the huge crowd of kids. It was seven o'clock, and from now on, for one night only this year as usual, the sedate town of Lewes, twenty minutes from Brighton, would be a good reconstruction of Bedlam. Packed trains would arrive from London on the hour; from Brighton three times as often. Shops would have shut early and the streets been closed to traffic hours ago; there wasn't a bed in town that didn't have someone's name on it or a pub seat that wasn't prebooked.

Long after the last train left for London at midnight, this genteel little joint would be a cross between Halloween and Mardi Gras as barrels of burning tar, thousands of fiery torch-bearing marchers dressed as Native Americans, Zulus, Vikings and Celtic Warriors and industrial-strength firework explosions would fill the steep and narrow streets – all leading to the awesome climax of the bonfire. There, an effigy of the Pope – accompanied at various times by a different dummy with a famous face – would be burned to deafening roars of approval. Because in 1556, seventeen Protestants were burned to death here under the orders of the Catholic queen, Bloody Mary.

And because it FEELS so good – to shout, to scream, to BRING IT ALL DOWN. Even I can see that, now. You can't forever be trying to keep stuff together. Sometimes it's the SENSIBLE thing – to destroy. And the first excess baggage I was set on getting shot of tonight was going to be boring, reliable old Kimmy, the Firefighters' Friend, hell-bent on checking smoke alarms not even her own like a thing possessed. No wonder Sugar felt smothered by me! I grabbed the vodka from her and swigged deeply, and was rewarded with a slick, skittering smile.

'Good girl!'

I tried to feel cherished by her approval. But I felt more like a poodle. I turned and looked out the window at the deepening purple of the Brighton suburbs flashing by, and I wondered if the people in those houses would ever know who I was. I felt myself frown, then, because thinking this felt weird. And then I realized that it felt weird simply because it was the first time in an age that I'd even considered a world beyond Sugar . . .

And then, just as fast as it had come back to me, that world flexed and warped and shimmered back into a shadowland once more. Because she had grabbed me by the shoulders and spun me round, and kissed me hard. In that packed, stacked, sweaty train carriage, full of hungry eyes and hormones and hysteria just waiting to happen. In the face of the full stifling force of teenage normality, she was showing her true colours . . .

I closed my eyes and kissed her back.

'WAAAY!' The lewd masculine cry went up en masse. For of course her colours such as they were were smeared wildly on a pirate flag, and her flag was a flag of convenience. I kept my eyes closed out of fear and loathing – for them, for her, but most of all for Dim Kim, who got straight As the way other teens got great Es, but who could also appar-

202

ently be taken for a ride up shit creek any old time. And I wondered why, after all this time, I was the slightest bit shocked to find that Maria's sexual fascination with me grew in inverse proportion to our privacy – that is, to our actual chance of DOING anything.

Sugar drew back; I finally opened my eyes, more resigned than repelled, to register her grand-standing smirk. Because things had changed, quelle surprise, to just the way she wanted. Before The Kiss, she'd merely been a beautiful teenage girl in a confined space where, let's face it, every fifth person was a beautiful teenage girl. But after The Kiss, she was the Top Girl. And all the other beautiful teenage girls, who had at a stroke been downsized into BORING beautiful teenage girls, looked at her with appalled admiration. The boys, though, looked at her with admiring appallment – a year ago, see, before SHE got to me, and saved me, and made me stupid, I'd have known. Anyway, I knew which look meant the most to her, which would ALWAYS mean the most – and certainly meant a lot more than the look on my face.

I looked at Sugar and laughed. She, the drunken dunce, thought that this meant I approved of the callous lunacy of her antics, and sniggered lewdly, nudging me in the ribs. Little did the she-creature know that I was actually laughing because I'd suddenly had a vision of her – the love of my so-called life – right smack-dab on top of the great Lewes bonfire, alongside the effigy of the Pope, burning away like billy-o. And not caring one bit, BECAUSE AT LEAST

SHE WAS THE CENTRE OF ATTENTION! Look at me, Ma – top of the world!

And I laughed again, imagining Suzy and She-Ra and Evil-Lyn and JJ gazing on in admiration, the dumb-asses, as their daughter/sister went up in flames, pouting and preening and sticking her tits out for the eternal lads. 'Ooh, 'Ria – you look just like Joan of Arc!'

'What you thinkin', Kizza?' she husked, nuzzling my ear as the boys phwooared on.

'Oh –' I favoured her with a dazzling, sincere smile; just for a moment, thanks to this vision, she had delighted me afresh, like in the beginning. 'Nothing really. Just that I'm never, ever going to check those bloody smoke alarms ever again –'

She looked puzzled for a moment, then joined with the cheer of King Mob as the train lurched to a stop. I sat there amid the bustle feeling strangely serene, until Maria tugged impatiently at my arm. 'Come on, Kiz – all the boys are getting off!'

I smirked up at her; I was a doll on a roll. 'How could they fail to, Sugar, when you're around?' I stood up, smiling smugly, and pushed past her.

End of the line.

'Remember, remember the fifth of November,
Gunpowder, treason and plot
I see no reason why gunpowder treason
Should ever be forgot!'

The Bonfire Boys sang out with the sort of pure, fierce, uncomplicated fervour that makes you realize it's no coincidence that men have their sex organs on the outside of their bodies, while women have them all concealed and complex. Much as I like girls, I couldn't help thinking that if one of us had written the famous Bonfire Night chant, the one that English kids grow up learning in nursery school the way they do altogether less exciting stuff about wandering goosey-gooseys and monarchy-ogling pussy cats, it'd be a lot more civilized but also a lot less rousing. Like, 'Let's all move on and agree to disagree/ On the issues which sparked the plot gunpowdery/ Protestant and Catholic, Muslim and Jew/ Let's share a veggie-sausage and prance round to U2!'

Rather than –

'Guy Fawkes, Guy Fawkes, he's intent
To blow up King and Par-luh-ment!
By God's providence he was catched
With a dark lantern and a burning match!'

Maria whooped and whistled and waved as the Grand United Procession passed by – two thousand people at least, dressed as Vikings and Aztecs and Zulus. They trundled burning tar barrels, they waved burning torches, they sang above the cacophony of a dozen marching bands which played different tunes yet moved to the beat of the same drum – timeless, shameless, blameless.

'So hollar boys, hollar boys, ring bells ring
HOLLAR BOYS, HOLLAR BOYS, GOD SAVE THE
KING!'

The word UNQUENCHED came into my mind unbidden and hung there in flames, and I seemed to go into a sort of trance for a minute or more. My throat was dry and my eyes were hot as I turned to Sugar to tell her I was sorry for dissing her, sorry for wishing her on top of a bonfire, to tell her that I was forever her friend in any way she wanted, vertical or horizontal – and saw her slipping through the snaky body of the march hand in hand with a tall blond boy wearing an almost-white bleached denim jacket, the back of which was emblazoned with the legend BRIGHTON TILL I DIE. Suddenly the phrase seemed to sum up all that was played-out and shut-in and washed-up about my hometown.

Like my love. My only love –
I followed them.

'A penny loaf to feed old Pope
A farthing cheese to choke him –'

Firework displays from five different directions illuminated my way as I followed that broad back and those long legs back up the High Street and through the narrow alleys, to the sound of the most bloodthirsty Lewes Bonfire 'prayer':

'A pint of beer to rinse it down
A faggot of sticks to burn him!'

I lost sight of Sugar and her stud, wheeled around frantically, then sighted them again by the green light of an exploding rocket. They were embracing in a way that made me marvel at how little difference there was between the physical appearance of true love and lying lust. I smiled painfully, and felt the casually vicious kick of old love, new heartburn or both; of course, with agonizing predictability, they were now passing under the tawdrily triumphant arch of an open-air car park.

'Burn him in a tub of tar!
BURN HIM LIKE A BLAZING STAR!'

I entered the car park and crept after them, dodging from the cover of car to car. And now, even above the fireworks, drums and voices, I could hear the unmistakable sound of sex – the to-ing and fro-ing, the yes-ing and no-ing, the giving in and giving up and giving tongue of that age-old thing known as Doing It. I heard it, I died inside and, ever conscientious, I raised my head to witness it –

And my always-wide eyes grew to manga dimensions as I saw not just the anticipated atrocity – Maria Sweet and A Boy on the bonnet of a car, HAVING SEX – but also another three boys, all at least eighteen, watching, smoking, laughing, WAITING.

In a heartbeat everything changed – how could I have

been so SELFISH? All this time moping over my diddums little hurted fweelings – and Sugar, my love, my friend, was being RAPED. Talk about a perspective injection! Why, it was practically MY FAULT – if I hadn't been giving her the silent treatment because of my hurt pride, she'd never have even gone off with this psycho . . .

Thank the Lord there were so many police around tonight; I'd crawl back to the car-park entrance, stand up and scream at them that I was about to fetch the law, then leg it and bring back help. They'd probably escape, but at least they'd let her go. And she could identify them later . . .

But just as I turned to go back, the BRIGHTON TILL I DIE boy lifted himself off her. She sat up, naked except for her trainers and crop top –

'Burn his body from his head
Then we'll say old Pope is dead!'

She smiled – and pushed her damp hair back from her sweating brow, and held her arms out to the next one –

'HIP HIP, HURRAH! HIP HIP, HURRAH! HIP HIP,
HURRAH!'

I ran.

16

I expect you're waiting for some sort of erotic-neurotic grand finale with me having the royal abdabs over what I saw that night. Well, DREAM ON.

When I saw Sugar . . . ENJOYING BEING GANG-BANGED that night, and I'm sorry if that sounds rude but, face it, it is pretty RUDE, having sex with four boys in a row on the bonnet of a car, even if it is a red Mercedes. Well, when I saw THAT little bit of business, as I walked away all numb, I didn't know where I was going or what I was doing. I was probably in shock. But then, I'd probably been in shock since Stella left, and it's not so bad. At least you don't get soppy mood swings – you're stable. So I just went with the flow along the High Street till I got to the War Memorial.

I was vaguely aware that people were counting down to midnight, and I thought they'd all just snog and shriek as usual. But then, as I was just about to start moping big-time, the sound of a trumpet playing 'The Last Post' rang out. And I know I should say that it 'rent' the sky or something, or 'split' it, but it did the opposite – it poured down over us like a glass and a half of full-cream milk, and suddenly we felt as perfect as chocolate. In the time it took to play those beautiful notes, both lush and stark at the same time, I think that at least two-thirds of the revellers there that night got some sort of take on our lives at last; that we really did have it easy, that life was wild and sweet, right here, right now, and that millions of people just as young and cute and clever as us had died, down the ages, to set us free – to see the fireworks and stay out late.

And the other third, well, they were having sex with Maria Sweet in a car park. With my Sugar – now THEIR Sugar. And tomorrow, someone else's Sugar, and so on, and so on, until she was so old and nasty that no one wanted her to be their Sugar any more. And at last, AT LAST I could see that THEY, the ones who had her now and would have her soon, were the ones who'd got the sticky end of the lollipop. And that, at the risk of being coarse, SugarWorld was no longer a place where I wanted to be.

The last note of 'The Last Post' faded and I turned southwards, towards the hard logic of the motorway and the sea. It was cold and dark and there were weird people out there in the big bad world, but I wasn't scared a bit. Because I was going home. And at last I knew the way.

It took me quite a while to get back to our house – OUR house, mine and Matt's and Dad's, NOT just the place where someone called Stella used to live, staring out of the window and picking at the skin around her nails, dreaming of a different life, refusing to grow up and making the rest of us old before our time because of it. We were better than that; I could see it so clearly now. I was going to go home, and I was going to do everything I could to re-invent my family. Rather than lose myself in LoveLand and leave the salvage job to Dad.

Then the sky was light and my feet were bleeding and Dad and Matt were all over me, yelling and laughing and scolding all at once. The words 'Young lady!' and 'Worried sick!' and 'Just about to call the police!' and 'You are SO grounded!' (from Matt; he was nearly eleven then, so allowed to crow) washed over me like a gallon of honey dumped in a hot tub as I drifted upstairs to the backing track of their irate joy. The last loving threat I remember was Dad shouting after me, 'And another thing, young lady – you are coming STRAIGHT out of that school! We haven't had a moment's peace since you've been there! And now your MOTHER, and not a moment too soon, has offered 500 pounds a month towards the extortionate up-keep of you two – and NO PRIZES for guessing what I'll be spending your half on. STRAIGHT back to the High! Oh yes, there'll be changes around here, make no mistake!'

He's SO great, my dad – so uncool that he's actually cutting edge, coming back the other way, right out there on his own. I remember laughing and calling back over my shoulder as I reached the top of the stairs, 'I love you all! All you little people! Thank you and goodnight!' And then, for the first time ever, literally LAUGHING myself to sleep, but softly, reflectively, not loudly and hysterically like a loon. I felt very young and vastly knowing and my own true age at last, all at once. The weight on my shoulders was gone. And tomorrow, to celebrate my new light-heartedness, I was going to take all the batteries out of our smoke alarms, just for kicks.

Just for an hour of course. During daylight. No need

211

to overdo it. It may have been a small step for your average teen – but it would be a giant one for Kim-kind.

It was weird being back at Preston High – nice weird though. Because AT LAST I WASN'T BORING ANY MORE. Teachers and kids alike knew about my Hard Times, my Lush Life – not just Ravendene (the Brighton teen equivalent of having Done Time in a really tough prison) but the Drugs Collapse Mercy Dash which had been so lavishly featured on the front page of the *Argus*. The school hallways I used to fret and worry down, or trail after Saint through, I strutted down now as though they were catwalks, forever in slo-mo, my triumphant blonde-ness flaring and swirling around my enigmatic smirk as I swung from class to class – always just a TINY BIT late, but nothing you could put your teacherly finger on; just the last girl to take her seat, smiling secretly – apparently lost in a world of my own which made their poor planet Earth look like some one-horse town.

My secret, and the source of my new strength, was simple; I was never, ever going to have a friend again. It was an easy decision to make, after what I'd been through. 'Friends' (aka 'fiends') had been the source of all my grief, from Saint to Sugar, and including Stella, whose insane conviction that it was better for all of us if she was my friend rather than my mother had surely made a sizeable contribution to her pissing off. Most people could be actually JAILED for hurting you. But friends . . . once you'd entered into that tragic kingdom, showed them your soft spots, and they'd sussed out who was the stronger one – SMELT it, like an animal smelling fear – they could do what they liked to you. Hurt you worse than anyone, because you'd trusted them with everything. We relax so completely with them, totally off our guard for once. And that's when they creep up behind us and strangle us with the friendship bracelet we made for them one sunny day so long ago.

I didn't think about Sugar as I settled back into my old school – why would I? She was just a sad, insecure bully who could only deal with worship or all-out war from people. I was Top Girl now, in my own way, hardened and hammered and honed with perfect aloneness. See, both Sugar and Saint thought they were hard, but they were both in their own way too soft, too NEEDY; Maria for the attention of boys, Zoe for the worship of girls. Frankly, they were both SO not a good look.

I was aware of that girl I used to know a lifetime ago, that Zoe Clements, saying something as I took stuff from my locker. I didn't bother to listen, just selected the books I needed, turned the key and turned to leave. But what do you know, the drip put her hand on my arm.

I just looked down at it, like I was trying to figure where it had come from, but didn't really give a flying one anyway. When she didn't take the hint and move it, I looked her in the face, smiled with my mouth but not my eyes and said 'Yes? Did you say something?'

'Kim . . .' She moved her hand down my arm and grabbed my wrist. I just carried on looking at it, sort of amused-bemused – I've gotta say it, this was about the coolest stroke I think I've ever pulled. 'I just said what I've been saying for the past two weeks. Just that I'm so glad you're back.' She licked her lips. 'And I'm so, so sorry I acted the way I did when you had to go to Ravendene. And when you were there. I was such a cow, so selfish, so thoughtless about what you were already going through, what with your mum going – makes me sick to think about it.'

'Don't beat yourself up,' I said pleasantly, remembering another thing I needed from my locker and unlocking it. 'Why, you'll probably have the chance to experience a broken home for yourself before long. Everyone knows what your dad's doing when he tells your mum he's playing golf. Talk about a hole in one. And he doesn't have any sort of handicap in that department, from what I've heard.' I looked at her stunned face and patted her shoulder softly. Of course, I was making it all up, but it could easily have been true. Her dad was a fox. And he'd always been so good to me. But I just didn't care any more.

I looked at her curiously from under my lashes; part of me wanted her to lose it and attack me, and I knew exactly what I'd do – go all passive and let her beat me up bad, and then she'd be expelled and basically screwed. I didn't want this PASSIONATELY or anything silly like that; I just thought it would be mildly amusing, to see a Golden Girl in meltdown. Another part of me wanted her to just be hurt and walk away. Hey, it's all good!

But do you know, I would have expected her to have

grown a pair of horns and gored me to death right there against the locker rather than do what she did next. She looked appalled, she flushed and bit her lip, she swallowed hard and then she said, 'I deserved that. And my dad, if he was here, he would STILL stick up for you, even after you dissed him like that. It was my dad made me see – see – what a bitch I've been.' She sighed and leaned against the lockers. 'He never says anything bad to me, you know that. But that night, when we were all here, when we got home he asked me to go for a walk with him. Just really quietly, and my dad's never quiet, so that scared the shit out of me for a start. And then we were just walking along Surrendon Road, and he started talking SO quietly to me, I had to lean in to hear him, and he was saying this . . . STUFF. Said what was the point in the last sixteen years, what had been the POINT in him and Mum – and he never gives her credit for anything, so THAT was scary too – taking such trouble trying to bring up a brilliant, beautiful, BLACK daughter – and he never says BLACK, so that was major creepy as well – who was a living, breathing rebuke to every crap stereotype about us being thuggy and careless and – I don't know, you know the type of thing. What people say. Not to me, but ABOUT US.

'He STOPPED there. He stopped there, because he was crying.' She gasped. 'He never cries, my dad. And then he turned away – he turned away –' (She was blubbing herself now.) '– and he told me to go home because he didn't want to look at me right now. And he just whispered that he never dreamed that his beautiful, brilliant black daughter would turn out to be less REAL, less of a PERSON, than the lowest, most ignorant piece of trailer trash –' She buried her face in her hands.

'Gosh, you really don't get it, do you, Zoe?' I said softly. 'Even during your big production number, the tear-jerking I-See-The-Light speech, you're STILL an ocean-going, Grade One BITCH. You're still talking about TRAILER TRASH!' I shut my locker again and turned the key. 'My mother may have been far from perfect. She may be conspicuous in her absence, even. But BEFORE she did a runner to Fantasy Island, she at least made me aware that we do not speak of our fellow human beings in such dehumanizing terms.' I smirked. It felt good to be Top Girl. 'Trailer trash – next comes white trash – and if white trash, why not black?' I hugged my books against my chest and sighed theatrically. 'You see, it's a slippery slope –'

She gaped at me through her tears, swallowed her pride, rubbed her eyes. 'I'm sorry. I've always had a problem with –'

Gosh, it was just like being on Oprah! I looked at my watch. 'Eat dirt, bitch,' I said politely. 'Which means your useless, empty words, for starters. Share it with your Po-Ho, if there's too much to swallow alone. Because I certainly have neither the time nor the inclination to join you at your trough of regret.' I put my head to one side, smiled briefly, shook my head. 'Zoe – empathy is like vitamin C; it doesn't keep. You have to put a bit in every day to keep a thing healthy. I needed your friendship way back when

– when my world fell down.' I shrugged. 'But my world's fine now. And your sympathy's just – and I mean this in a CARING sort of way – like some dead weight on my back.' I turned to go, and saw that quite an audience had gathered. It WAS like Oprah!

I heard more snivelling, would you believe, and felt her hand on my shoulder. 'Kimmy –'

I turned back and smiled like a crocodile near the end of its tether; I had to do something drastic to get this sodden stalker off my case. I thought fast.

'Zoe. I always wanted to tell you something. But you were my friend, and I was too nice. But now you're not, and I'm not –'

'What?' she mumbled.

I searched wildly for something nasty to say. The real stuff, like she was lacking in empathy and up herself, she'd defused by admitting to. Then I had it! Just the thing she used to say about other girls, back when she was uncorrupted by compassion.

'You SMELL,' I lied earnestly. 'Maybe it's the sports, maybe it's the smoking, maybe it's the smugness. But you smell quite bad really, often worse than the poor hangers you actually accuse of smelling. And the reason why no one's ever told you in all these years, not even Chloe Feinstein whose life you've made a misery marathon, is BECAUSE YOU'RE BLACK.'

I walked away. There was silence – I counted to five – then a wail.

'But you said NO ONE EVEN NOTICED my

colour! Because I was so pretty! LIKE SAMANTHA MUMBA!'

'I WAS LYING!' I lied loudly over my shoulder. 'TO BE NICE!'

And with that, I walked on by. Man, I was BAAAD. And it felt GOOOD.

It hadn't worked, quelle surprise, the attempted hooking-up and harmonization of our savagely divided town's rich and poor through the medium of Brighton schools; at least, not for Preston High and Ravendene Comp. Word had it that the Ravers were about to be disbanded alto-gether and sent their separate ways, so bad was the rep of the school; I wouldn't be sad or anything soppy about its demise, but I did smile sardonically (I hope) when I heard about it, knowing that a part of Brighton's tribal under-belly would be gone forever. Without the Ravers united, would the Little Beirut of West Street on a Saturday night ever be the same?

This winter afternoon was to be the last time that we prissy Prestoners – the flowering future leaders of our island home! – graced Ravendene with our presence.

The forthcoming demise of the snob/yob integration scheme may have been a step backwards for socialism, but let's face it, it was a hop, skip and a jump for me re the Sugar situation. I mean, I didn't LOVE her any more or anything girly like that, but on the other hand I didn't need her in my face.

And there she was, waiting for the bus to arrive, with a sort of wistful, slightly hungry look – like some old Albanian babushka waiting for the UN gravy train or something. She came forward, smiling hesitantly as I climbed down.

'Come for one last smoke then, Kizzy?'

As we walked silently out on to the playground, I looked sideways at Maria Sweet and, for the first time, I didn't see her. I saw her mother – sweet, silly, careless to the point of self-immolation. I saw JJ – sexy and flash as a firefly, fated to flare up and die inside before he even knew what it was like to really live. I saw She-Ra and Evil-Lyn – name-calling, tongue-poking imps. But no longer did I see THAT THING in her, the thing that had made me toss and turn and burn –

'Jesus!' said a familiar voice from behind us as we lit up. 'Are you STILL trying to take her down with you? Can't you see she's right back out of your league now, for good? Just leave her!' It was Clements; she'd followed us, the weirdo, right from the bus.

Maria sneered and blew smoke in her face. 'Aw, fuck off back to your own stuck-up school, will you, Nosebag?'

'With pleasure! It can't come soon enough for me, frankly. But sadly, we've got to spend one last afternoon in this dump – and the last thing Kimberly needs is you foisting your drugs on her. D'you KNOW what's gonna happen to her if they catch her using again? SHE'LL GET KICKED OUT! SHE WON'T BE ABLE TO DO HER EXAMS!'

'MY NAME'S NOT KIMBERLY!' I yelled. 'YOU DON'T EVEN KNOW MY NAME!' I knew she was speaking the truth – but she should have known my name if she wanted me to listen to her. I felt mad as hell and reached out to grab the joint from Sugar's hand, inhaling deeply before passing it back.

'You got any more?' I demanded.

'Coupla joints –'

'Give them –' I grabbed them and put them into my bookbag. 'I'll pay you later –'

'You DUMB cow!' Saint exploded. 'And of course you'll end up SHARING them with her! Which makes you her MULE!'

'Better than being your dog!' I hissed. 'Now fuck off back to class, like a good little bitch!'

We watched her go. Her head was down and she moved gracelessly, like her legs were tired and heavy, for the first time I could ever recall. 'Don't look so glossy now, does she?' Sugar smirked.

'Oh, shuddup.' She just made me feel tired. Everything did. 'I don't need you either. Let's just get in there and have the whole thing done with.'

We trudged back across the playing field. 'So you're back in the swing at Preston then?'

'Yup.'

'Am I gonna see you?'

I laughed. 'Why start now!'

'Aw, Kim . . . don't be like that.'

'Maria, I'm not like anything. That's my trouble. I'm

just this empty, vacant . . . THING that just stands around waiting for people with actual PERSONALITY to, I don't know, fill me up or something. Shine their light on me and make me real for a while. 'Cept it doesn't really. It makes me less real each time. And each time this big searchlight person, like Saint or you, takes the light away from me, I'm just a weaker and weaker copy of my real self. Like a Xerox of a Xerox. And one day, all that's going to be left of me are these faint squiggles where you can't even make out my name. And then I really won't stand a chance of making anything. Of being anything.'

I stopped and stared searchingly into her face one last time. I had to try to make her understand what it was like to be ordinary, to not be a real Top Girl. If nothing else would stand to prove that our love ever existed, this comprehension, this empathy, would at least be a decent memorial.

She stared deep into my eyes, her beautiful untroubled babyish brow furrowed in thought AT LAST, and then she spoke –

'Kim, d'you think I should grow out my fringe – or would it make me look weird, cos of my big forehead, like an alien or summat?'

I couldn't believe it. But WHY couldn't I believe it? – it was just Sugar, BEING SUGAR. She wasn't being weird – I was, expecting her to be different. I laughed softly and shook my head. 'You are an alien, Maria. You'll never be normal. Thank God.'

*

221

I like dogs; I always wanted us to get one, but for as long as I can remember, Dad has said he just didn't 'get' it – the 'pet thing'. He was like, thirty-nine pence a day for a tin of Kennomeat – what's in it for me? He never said that, but you could tell he was thinking it. It was weird that he was so intent on making our house a 'home', yet didn't see the blinding fact that a licky, barky sort of character could have done in two shakes of his tail what any number of earthenware jars with French words for food on them didn't achieve in a decade or more. Dogs have always liked me too; I mean, they're DOGS, I know they like most people, but I still maintain that they like me that extra bit. Face it, they probably sense that I'm just as pathetically friendly and bossable, just as TAIL-WAGGY as them.

This dog liked me – the one who looked me straight in the face as I walked into my last class at Ravendene. He was a silky-eared spaniel with eyes like hot toddies, and under different circumstances I'm sure I'd have liked him too. But as things were, his best friend appeared to be a policeman.

And I was carrying drugs. Those two lousy joints, I realized with a sudden sickening plummet to the stomach, meant that there was a very good chance indeed of my whole future life going right down the toilet.

Behind me, I felt Maria fade away.

They say people get to look like their dogs. I don't know if the young policeman who was also staring at me had silky ears, but he certainly had hot-toddy eyes, wide and beautiful in his satiny-skinned, Latin-looking face. He smiled then, and gestured towards the floor by the black-board. There were two dozen bookbags, all in a row.

'Hello, miss. Can you put your bag down, please. Right there, at the end of the row. Then take a seat.'

I walked forward, put it down. Turned to the class. Was vaguely aware of Saint's stricken face as I took a seat in front of her.

'Right you are,' the beautiful policeman nodded. He was looking straight at me. 'And for our latecomer, may I introduce my friend – PC Scooby-Don't.'

The class laughed uneasily; the spaniel wagged his tail happily. I didn't do either.

'PC Scooby is your friend too,' the policeman droned. Lying bastard. 'A friend who wants to help you. Who wants to empower you, so you can make clear, informed decisions about your future.' Then he snapped his head round, and he and PC Scooby locked eyes and pricked ears. Suddenly, you could almost SMELL the bond of power-madness that linked them. 'PC Scooby-Don't – SEARCH!'

Of course, you know what happened next. The bastard barker went STRAIGHT to my bag and after a quick sniff just sat there, yapping and wagging. The rotten rozzer strode up to him, picked my bag up, put in his hand and, wouldn't you know it, pulled out Exhibits A and B.

All eyes were on me, except the dog's. He stared madly at his master and was rewarded with some dirty-looking chew, slipped to him casually by the architect of my ruin. I can't deny that I felt very bitter towards PC Scooby at that moment; if his reward for shopping me had been a decent bit of sirloin it wouldn't have seemed so bad, but to think that my entire future was riding on a mouldy bit of, I don't know, COW HIDE, was the final straw.

I opened my mouth; nothing came out. I tried again. And then I heard a voice. But not my own.

'It's mine,' said Zoe Clements. Then she cleared her throat and her chair scraped as she stood up and said it again. 'IT'S MINE.'

'Why is it in this young lady's bag, then?' He didn't believe her.

'Because I saw the dog. And you. And I knew what was going to happen.' She was in control of herself now, sounding cool and just a little amused. 'And I'd had a – a row with Kim. I wanted to get her into trouble. People saw us –' I heard her swallow, make a big effort. 'People saw me crying –'

I sensed her looking around the room, sure of support. And right on cue the Preston girls murmured their assent; our audience at the lockers.

'I see.' The policeman stared at her, looked right through her. He didn't believe her – but she would never back down, and he could never prove it. I knew that now, as surely as I knew my own name – K.I.M. And I knew, amazingly, that the worst thing I could do would be to stand up and deny her her perfect moment. The bruising she had been cruising for all her life. The thing that would make everything right – leave her with a clean slate, to be every brilliant thing she could be. To make her dad proud.

'Will you come with me, miss?'

As she passed by me she put her hand on my shoulder. I looked up at her and I saw fear in her eyes. I panicked then – opened my mouth to speak, to tell the truth. But she shook her head sharply.

'I'm sorry, Kim.'

17

I only saw Sugar once in my life after that day, and it was the strangest thing. I was squaring up to my A Levels and it was early summer and I was lying on my back in St Ann's Well Gardens, reading Dr Faustus. Or trying to –

Because suddenly Saint was back on the scene after a long period of exile in Trinidad, and she was shouting down her mobey a mile a minute as she triumphantly fielded congratulations on her Olympic-sprint confirmation. When there was a minute's respite, I closed my book and said to her, 'Turn it off for a bit.'

'Why? – oh, OK.' She was different now, see. 'But can't I at least keep it on vibrate?' She twinkled at me. 'And, like, sit on it –?'

I sat up. 'Just for a moment. I wanted to say something –'

'Ooh.' She mock-shuddered. 'It's just like Oprah, innit –'

'I just wanted to say – you know – thank you –'

She shrugged. 'Forget it – you did me a favour. That "my brilliant career" thing – it was gettin' OLD.'

'How come you're allowed in the Olympics though, when you were chucked out of school on a drugs rap?'

She hooted, and grabbed the top of her right arm with her left hand. 'My coach took blood, obviously. OBVIOUSLY he wasn't going to convict me on my own lying word like the school did, because he, um, like BELIEVES in me? He's known me since I was young –'

I felt a sickness that was almost like love, but without the sweetness to heal it. 'So have I, Saint . . .'

'Yeah . . . but not REALLY known me, perhaps. And, y'know, maybe that wasn't your fault. With me, then – well, maybe, what was there to know –'

She looked away and I moved to touch her arm and tell her that none of that mattered any more, because now we were all grown up, when suddenly she turned sharply and pinched my thigh where my cut-offs ended. It took me so much back to when we were fifteen that I instinctively punched her, but she pushed me down on to the grass and put her hand over my mouth.

A tall, dark and handsome young couple were passing along the path that separated the grass from the tennis courts, the girl pushing a pram. Even before I could hear their words I sensed the frequency of a squabble – but not a fight, or even a row. Even in their disagreement, they were bound and shielded by the shimmer of love.

'Well, you know, like SUE ME, but I don't happen to think that the name RENATA is particularly PLAIN –'

'Well, then there's Jane –'

'With a Y?'

The boy laughed and took control of the pram in one smooth move. 'No! We're not bringing up no lap dancer here –'

'I'm not calling no kid of mine Jane, Y or not. Jane's OK for some rich kid who don't need to prove nothing – not HER –'

'Maria . . .' The young man's voice was patient and

almost amused, but not quite, because that would be insulting to her, the way he saw it. But he wasn't going to back down. 'Call the baby Susan after your mother. Call her Catherine after mine – Kate. Call her Renata or Jane. But you are NOT going to call her Kim –'

I went to sit up again – Saint pushed me back, shushing, smiling down on me as she covered my all-too-human body with her superior Olympic-class one.

'Well, why not! It's PLAIN, if you like –'

'It's NOT plain.' Mark Wood stopped walking and frowned at his wife just slightly, not angry, just puzzled she didn't understand yet. 'Kim sounds plain, because it's short, but it's VAIN. And above all, it's a PRETTY girl's name. You'll never meet a plain Kim.' He looked down into the pram. 'Obviously she's gonna BE pretty – but I don't want that to be her THING. It's bad for girls. D'you see?'

Maria sighed, and bent towards the baby, tucking it in or something. 'I'm trying to, Mark.'

They walked on slowly.

'What about Zoe?' said Mark.

Our eyes widened in delighted amazement as we lay there not three metres away from them.

'ZOE!' Maria sneered. And for a moment it all came flooding back, for all three of us. 'As if!' Then she stopped, and looked puzzled. Then she smiled up at him. 'ZOE. Come to think of it, I like it. I really do!' She took the pram back firmly. 'What's it mean?'

'It means life.' Mark kissed the top of her head as they

228

walked on. 'It might even be pagan actually, but I like it. And I like its meaning.'

'Well – can't argue with that.' Maria laughed in delight, and in that moment I knew that against all odds she was born again in bliss – that everything would be shiny for her. And with that she walked on out of my life forever.

I looked up at Zoe – MY Zoe. And suddenly I got it. See, whatever you THOUGHT you wanted from life, whatever you thought you were going to BE, it's pretty sure that someone got stuff muddled at source. And it probably wasn't even their fault. In the papers you see mothers who got the wrong baby and it's meant to be the exception to the rule, but who knows? It's entirely likely, human fallibility being what it is, that someone else entirely has got your WHOLE LIFE. And good luck to them too, and good for you, because chances are they'll end up taking better care of it than you would.

Than I did.

But tell you what, I think at least I've worked out about LOVE now, which isn't SO bad for seventeen, a BIT sad but sort of sweet too. What I think is, it's like walking across a high wire, without a safety net. If you're a bit lucky, you get from one side to the other. But if you're REALLY lucky, REALLY REALLY lucky, you fall off –

And you fly –

So we were quiet for ages then, just thinking about all those years we'd already had together, without knowing. Were they behind us, or between us? Was it going to be easier or harder, that we already knew everything about each other? Except that one thing . . .

'So.' I finally found my voice; it sounded surprisingly calm and cool – and if I say so myself, just a LITTLE bit sexy. 'DOES Zoe mean life?'

She stroked my hair and looked at me gravely. 'I guess. It COULD. Some other life than what I imagined. But perhaps EXACTLY the life I dreamed.'

I was reeling. And for the first time I understood the word 'smote'. Like in the Bible, the made-up mad bits, when some sad bro kills his homie. I wasn't 'smitten', because that could stop and I would still live. Not this, though. I was totally, TOTALLY smote.

'Saint.' I swallowed. 'I need your input here.' I coughed slightly in her face; she tut-tutted. She'd never change. Except in the biggest and best of ways.

'Kimbo –'

I had to say it now. At last. 'Do you, like, LOVE me?'

'Here. Kimbo.' She tucked my hair behind my ear, traced the snub of my nose, took my chin in her hand and whispered in my ear just before she kissed me. 'Here, Kimbo – was Goofy a dog?'